THE CHALLENGE

"I've heard a lot of stories about you, Abbot," I said. "I don't know what to believe."

"Don't believe any of 'em," he said. "I'm the most-lied-about man in Miles City."

"What about the story that you're the biggest man in the country and you don't like to be crossed?"

This was good enough for openers. Abbot was confused. I had trouble identifying him as the subject of the worst stories I'd heard, but I knew that appearances don't tell anything about a man.

"Just why did you come in here?" Abbot demanded after a long pause.

"Mostly to find out where you stand," I said. "If I'm going to be marshal, I aim to run my department. I've heard that you expect to give orders."

"All right," Abbot said. "I'll tell you straight out that I think we hired the wrong man. I think you're too tough and too strict and I think you'll be dead before Christmas if you stay on the job."

THE LAW AT
MILES CITY

Wayne D. Overholser

LEISURE BOOKS NEW YORK CITY

A LEISURE BOOK®

July 2005

Published by special arrangement with Golden West Literary Agency.

Dorchester Publishing Co., Inc.
200 Madison Avenue
New York, NY 10016

ISBN 0-8439-5556-2

The name "Leisure Books" and the stylized "L" with design are trademarks of Dorchester Publishing Co., Inc.

Printed in the United States of America.

Visit us on the web at www.dorchesterpub.com.

THE LAW AT MILES CITY

Chapter One

Two things about life have always puzzled me. First, in a normal span of three score years and ten a man will meet thousands of people. Most of them remain casual acquaintances, perhaps so casual he may not even know their names, but out of those thousands one or two or three will play a big part in his life. In my case there were three: Jeffrey Munro, Pete Green, and Sandra Lennon.

The second thing is that every person has one or two or three experiences in which he lives in the eye of the storm, a sort of Gethsemane, or perhaps Waterloo would be a better term. In my case there was one event, and in my case the three people and the event were closely related.

I was twenty-five the day I rode into Miles City, or Milestown as it was first known. I had left home when I was twelve, a home that had never been a real home because I'd lived with my grandparents in eastern Kansas since I was three. I don't think any love for me was involved. My mother and father had died of malaria and there wasn't anyone else to take me.

My grandparents were old and crotchety, and I was a burden to them. I wasn't mean, but I was ornery, and I have a notion they were as glad when I left as I was glad to be leaving. I knocked around all over the West from the Colorado mining camps to the Williamette Valley farms in western Oregon.

In the course of those thirteen years there wasn't much in the way of work I didn't do. I was hungry and cold plenty of times. I met all kinds of people, from the worst and most brutal outlaws to some fine human beings. I took a complete course in the college of hard knocks and graduated with honors. Although I was bitter at times about my life, there were other times when I was happy and satisfied and never gave a thought to the future.

Before I rode into Miles City, I had spent a year in Clearwater, which was located about 100 miles above Miles City. It was a tough town populated by hide hunters and drifters and outlaws who were looking for a safe place to hole up. There were soldiers, too, from a nearby fort, and now and then a band of Indians would camp near town.

I was hired as town marshal because no one else was crazy enough to take the job. I took it because I was broke and hungry, and at the moment I didn't much care whether I lived long enough to see my twenty-fifth birthday or not. I had served as a lawman before, but never for a very long period and never in a difficult situation. For me it was a case of sink or swim, and somehow I swam.

When I left Clearwater, I was not aware I had made myself a reputation as a town tamer. While I was there, I killed two men and busted up more than I can remember. I was six-feet-two. I weighed just under 200 pounds, and necessity taught me to use my strength and be as mean and brutal as I had to be to get the job done.

The day I rode out of town I had money in my pocket and a stomach full of drunks and hardcases who didn't respect anything except a hard fist on their jaw or a gun muzzle against their guts. I soon found out I did have a reputation of sorts when I stopped in the small towns along the river or met someone on the road and told them I was Dave Harmon. Nine times out of ten the man would say—"Oh, you're the marshal who tamed Clearwater."—or something like that. I wasn't proud of my reputation, but I wasn't ashamed of it, either.

I didn't have any real goal in mind when I rode into Miles City. I was just drifting, thinking vaguely that I'd stay here a few days, and, if I didn't find anything I wanted, I'd go on to the Black Hills. Settling down wasn't in my mind at all; a wife and children were the last things I wanted.

I rode past Fort Keogh, which had been built shortly after the battle of the Little Big Horn, then across the military bridge that spanned the Tongue River. I was in Miles City then. It wasn't much of a town, but then I hadn't expected much. There were the usual wide Main Street, the hitch rails, the boardwalks, and the false-fronted log buildings filled with a variety of businesses, from blacksmith shops and livery stables to hardware and drug stores.

This was August 10, 1881, a hot, sultry day with dust deep on Main Street, a few dogs sleeping in whatever shade they could find, and a dozen or so chickens scratching in the manure in front of the livery stable, but no people. It was, I thought, a deserted town. I left my horse at the Diamond D Corral, asking: "Any people live here?"

The stableman grinned. "A few. They just don't like the heat on a day like this."

I wiped my face with my bandanna, not blaming them one bit. I took a room in a hotel, or what passed as a hotel, and, when I returned to Main Street, I saw that it was still empty. I thought I might as well go on to the Black Hills in the morning, that there was nothing here to hold me. *No hurry,* I thought. I was tired and hot and sweaty. I was also dry, so I stepped into Wolf's Saloon and ordered a drink.

The saloon wasn't much cooler than it was in the street. One man was standing at the bar talking to the bartender. A poker game was going on near the windows. One of the players had a woman standing behind him. He was obviously a professional gambler dressed in a black coat, a ruffled white shirt, and a black string tie. Three men were talking and drinking at a table in the back. That was all, but it was the most people I had seen since I'd ridden into Miles City.

I nursed my drink for a few minutes, thinking this was about as dead a town as I'd ever seen in my life. For a time I paid no attention to the man at the bar until I heard the bartender say: "Yes, Mister Munro."

It wasn't often that a bartender showed that much respect for a customer, so I gave this Mr. Munro a good looking over. He was bigger than I was, outweighing me by at least fifty pounds, and he was a couple of inches taller. I judged he was about fifty. He had all the marks of a working cowhand about him, but there was something about the man that said he was no ordinary thirty-a-month-and-beans cowboy.

I puzzled over that a minute or two, thinking I had learned something about people in the year I'd carried a star in Clearwater. It was a matter of necessity because it's never smart to mistake an outlaw for an honest citizen. Not that any man can tell for sure, but I'd learned a few hints. I'd also learned some things about the man who owns a ranch or a business, or at least has risen a notch or two above the ordinary John Doe citizen.

The frontier has always been famous for the equality of its people, but the fact remains that there were a few men who had money or property, and for that reason swung a little more weight than a working man. As I said, I'm not always sure just what it is that sets these men aside in the eyes of a sharp observer. Maybe it's the way they hold their shoulders or the way they wear their hats, or perhaps the tone of their voices. Or, in Munro's case, maybe it was his beautiful red beard and mustache. Or it may have been nothing more tangible than the fact that he looked like a man who gave orders. Whatever it was, I judged the man to be someone of importance, and I wondered about him.

Probably I'd have finished my drink and walked out of the saloon and that would have been the end of my relationship with Munro, if he hadn't said: "Damn it, quit calling me Mister Munro. My name's Jeff."

I knew then, and wondered why I hadn't pegged him before. Jeff Munro was a pioneer in Montana, going back to the boom days of Alder Gulch and Bannack. He had been a member of the Vigilantes that cleaned up the Plummer gang. He'd hit it lucky at Alder Gulch, then moved north to Deer Lodge and run a business of some kind. He'd served in the Territorial Legislature. The last thing I'd heard of him was that he'd brought in a big herd of Oregon cattle and started a ranch in the Judith Basin.

I couldn't even guess why he was in Miles City and I didn't care. I figured he'd be riding on and I'd never see him again, and I wanted to shake hands with him. I've never been a hero-worshiper and I didn't intend to be then, but I honestly admired Jeff Munro, so I picked up my drink and moved along the bar toward him.

He glanced at me, curious, I guess. The bartender turned away to serve a customer who had just come in from the street. I held out my hand and said: "I've heard of Jeff Munro, ever since I got to Montana. I want to shake hands with you."

He laughed shortly and gripped my hand, but he was cool. I don't know what he thought or how he pegged me. I suppose he had a right to be suspicious and that any man as well known as Jeff Munro was subject to all kinds of con games. Anyhow, it was plain enough that he wasn't extending himself to a stranger.

"I can think of a lot of men who would like to do something more to me than shake my hand," he said. "Now, who are you?"

I got red in the face, ashamed that I hadn't introduced myself. I said: "I'm Dave Harmon. I guess I forgot to tell you who I am."

"Dave Harmon," he said, suddenly thawing. "You're the man who cleaned up Clearwater, ain't you? What are you doing in Miles City? Come after a prisoner?"

I shook my head. "I quit. I'm headed down the river. I had enough of Clearwater. I'm just seeing the country."

"Not much to see around here," he said. "I rode in from the Judith Basin a couple of days ago. I'd like to start another ranch down here somewhere, but I haven't seen a ranch site I like. Tomorrow I'm taking a sashay up the Tongue River, and I'll circle back down the Rosebud."

"I've never been in that country," I said.

"Neither have I," he said. "If I don't find anything I like, I'll go back and forget about another ranch. I've got about all I can handle anyway." He fished a cigar out of his pocket and rolled it between his fingertips. "You know, Harmon, right now a lot of Montana is waiting for somebody to claim it. We'll have hundreds of big herds moving in here within the next five years. By that time there won't be a good ranch site left in the territory. Another year or two and the buffalo will be gone and we'll have cows crowding every range from the Dakotas to Idaho."

I blinked a little at that. It was hard for me to see a wilderness like Montana being settled within the next five years, and it took me a while to get used to the idea. Then I said: "Well, the buffalo will be gone, and that's a fact. I hate to see it."

"It'll keep the Indians on the reservations," he said, as if he wasn't sure that was a good thing. "Nothing has ever held the pioneers back in this country from any place where there was free land, and Montana has got that. It ain't good for

12

much except range, but I reckon some idiots will plow the grass up and try to raise grain."

"They've tried before," I said. "Chances are they'll try again."

He studied me for a moment, then he said: "If I was a young man, I'd think about settling down here in Miles City. It's going to be a good town, another Dodge City. The herds coming north from Texas will drive down the Tongue. A railroad's bound to come across Montana and go on to the coast, and it'll go through Miles City." He shrugged. "It may be a locoed dream, but I've got a hunch that Miles City will be the best town in eastern Montana."

"Are you going to invest here?" I asked.

He laughed. "I've invested a little, but I wish I had some big money to invest." He shook his head. "No, I've got some partners who want another ranch. They've got the money and I've got the savvy, but I'd never convince them that a new town like Miles City is a good place to invest. All they can think of is cows. If I'm reading the sign right, in another ten years we'll be overshooting the mark with cows on the Western ranges."

I stood there for a minute, thinking he'd given me a good deal to chew over. Miles City wasn't much right then, but who knew what it might be in five years? Or ten? It was time that I started giving some thought to the future. I'd seen too many men drift all their lives and end up old men, swamping out saloons or having to beg a living from anybody they could. I didn't intend to wind up that way.

"Maybe I ought to look around here," I said. "I guess I'll go out and explore the town. Hard to tell what opportunities are waiting for me."

"That's right," he said. "I'll see you before I leave town."

I started for the street door, vaguely aware that the three

men, who had been sitting at the back table, were on their feet. I was thinking my own thoughts and didn't pay any attention to them until I heard the solid thud of fist on flesh.

I wheeled around. Those three bastards had headed straight for Jeff Munro. Two of them had grabbed him by the shoulders and arms and had jammed him against the bar, and the third man was giving him a hell of a pounding.

Munro was heaving and twisting and kicking, but he wasn't doing much good. Three men were too many. I started toward them, knowing this wasn't my fight, but I also knew I couldn't stay out of it.

They were so busy with Munro they didn't know I was anywhere around there until I grabbed the man who was doing the hitting. I whirled him around and let him have it on the jaw. It was a beautiful punch, one of the best I ever threw. He went back, and his knees gave under him, and he spilled out flat on the floor and lay there.

The other two men whirled to take me. I ducked a wild punch from one of them and caught him in the guts. I heard the wind whoosh out of him, and he bent over, holding his belly. Then the roof fell on me. I went down on my hands and knees. I wasn't out cold, but I couldn't move. I heard a man say—"Kill him!"—and I knew damned well there wasn't anything I could do to stop them.

Chapter Two

A gun went off. I was so muddle-headed that for a few seconds I thought one of the hardcases had tried to shoot me and missed, but then I realized that the gun had been fired by someone standing on the window side of the room, not along the bar. I finally got my head turned enough to see that one of the poker players was on his feet, a gun in his hand. It was the gambler who'd had the woman standing behind him.

"You, there!" the gambler called. "You two sons-of-bitches were working Munro over. I hope you'll make a move for your guns. I want an excuse to kill both of you."

By this time I was thinking a little straighter. I discovered that I could move my hands and legs, so I crawled to the bar and pulled myself to my feet. I thought my head was going to split wide open, and I also thought I was going to faint, but neither happened.

The gambler said: "All right, if you're not going to give me an excuse to kill you, get away from the bar and hook the moon. Any time you feel like going for your guns, just go ahead and try."

Apparently they had no intention of committing suicide, so they obeyed. The one I'd knocked out was still on the floor, not moving. Munro had backed up against the bar. He was bent over and holding his hands against his belly. He was still having trouble breathing, and blood was running down his chin from his nose. The man the gambler had shot was lying on his belly between me and the door. He looked dead to me, but I was in no shape to find out for sure. At the moment I didn't much care.

"Abe," the gambler called, "go fetch the marshal! Lane, you get the doc." He motioned to the woman. "Lucky, go help our friend to a chair. He should be sitting down."

The woman crossed the room to me. She was tall and well-built, about thirty, I judged, and even in my dazed condition I was aware that she was a fine-looking woman. She said: "Lean on me. You can make it to the chair."

I made it, and I certainly leaned on her. My head was hurting as much as ever, and I thought I was going to pitch forward on my face the instant I started walking toward the chair, but she held me up, and I sat down. I felt better as soon as I got off my feet.

The woman patted me on the shoulder. "Stay there. You took a gun barrel across the top of your head. Don't walk until the doctor gets here."

"Thank you," I said, but the words didn't come out with much steam.

The gambler edged toward me, holding his gun on the two toughs. When he reached me, he said: "I'm Pete Green. I was about to take chips in the game when you horned in. I don't owe Jeff Munro anything, but it goes against my grain to see one man take a beating from three. When this fourth man moved up and slugged you, I decided it was time to sit in on their game."

"They were going to kill you," the woman said. "The one who hit you had cocked his gun and was lining it on your head when Pete shot him."

I held out my hand to Green. "I'm Dave Harmon," I said. "How do you thank a man for saving your life?"

"You don't," he said. "Just write it down in the book. There may be a day when I'll need some help."

"All right," I said. "I'll do that."

The doctor came in then, a small, bearded man who took a

look at Munro and said: "Go across the street to my office. I'll be there in a minute." He knelt beside the man Green had shot and felt for his pulse. He got up, shaking his head. "I'll move the body to my place in a little while, Luke." He nodded at one of the poker players. "See that I get a coffin this evening. This jasper's a stranger to me. Any of you know him?"

"No," Green said.

"They're all strangers," the bartender said. "I never seen any of 'em till today."

The doctor came to me. "What happened to you?"

"I caught a gun barrel across my noggin," I told him.

"Good thing you had your hat on," he said. "Take it off."

I did. The doctor felt of my head, and then stepped back. "Not much I can do for you, my friend. If we had some way of taking a picture of the bones in your skull, we could tell what damage was done, but we don't, so all I can tell you is to go to bed and stay flat on your back for a while. You'll have a headache, and you're going to have the world spinning around in front of you when you first get up after you've been lying down. You're just going to have to let nature do some healing. It may be quite a while before you get clear over this."

He walked out of the saloon just as the marshal came in. The man I'd knocked out had come around and was sitting up. Green said: "Take these three men to jail for assault and battery, Bill. If you figure that's not enough to arrest them for, make it attempted murder."

"That's a damned lie!" one of the men yelled. "You're the one who just murdered a man." He pointed to the body. "Look at him, Marshal. This bastard shot him."

Green walked to the man and slapped him hard on the side of the face. "If it's murder you want," he said, "you'll get it, if

17

you keep shooting off your mouth."

The marshal drew his gun and motioned for the man I'd knocked out to line up beside the other two. He asked: "How'd you happen to shoot this one, Pete?"

"Three of them jumped Jeff Munro," Green said. "Then Harmon here moved in and was handling them three pretty good when that one"—he motioned to the dead man—"slugged Harmon from behind with a gun barrel. He was fixing to shoot Harmon when I let him have it. I think you'll find all four of them are wanted men."

The lawman nodded. "Probably."

"If you have any doubts about what I've told you," Green said, "go over to the doc's office and look at Munro."

"I might do that," the marshal said, then turned to me. "You Dave Harmon, the Clearwater marshal?"

"I'm Dave Harmon," I said, "but I'm not the Clearwater marshal. I resigned."

"Looking for a marshal's job?" he asked.

"No."

"Too bad," he said. "You could have one here for the asking." He turned to the three prisoners and nodded at the door. "Move. Out through the front, then turn left."

When they were gone, Green said: "I've got to get back to the game. Lucky, you go with Harmon to his room. Stay with him and make him comfortable."

She put a hand to my shoulder. "I'm a good nurse," she said. "I'll keep you company for a while."

I made it into the street, the hot sunlight hitting me like a blast from an overhead furnace. I put a hand against the wall, the street pinwheeling in front of me. The woman held my other arm, and stayed there until the dizziness passed.

"Keep trying," she said. "Stay on your feet."

I did. I've had my share of fights and I've been banged up

considerably, but I had never felt like that before. Somehow I made it to my room. I had a tough time getting up the stairs. I held to the banister with one hand, taking a step at a time, and resting between each one.

The woman kept holding to my other arm. The instant I reached my room, I spilled across the bed and lay there. After a short time the throbbing eased off and the pain became less severe. The woman tugged at my boots and finally got them off, then she unbuckled my gun belt.

"Roll over," she said. "Far enough so I can pull your belt free."

I didn't want to move, but I did, the hammering inside my skull starting as soon as I began to turn. I rolled back and stared at the ceiling, biting my lower lip to keep from groaning. The women poured water from the pitcher into the wash basin, wet a towel, wrung it out, and, coming to me, laid it across my forehead.

"You don't have to stay here," I said.

"Don't you want my company?" she asked.

"Sure," I said, "only I'm not what you'd call good company."

"That's all right," she said, smiling. "I don't have to have good company. As a matter of fact, Pete isn't good company anytime he has a losing streak. I'm used to it."

"What's your name?"

"Lucky."

"Lucky what?"

"Not Lucky What." She laughed. "Just Lucky. I'm living in sin with Pete. Maybe he'll marry me someday. Maybe not. Or maybe he'll walk off and leave me. It's never made much difference to me. I've got a living with him. As far as the decent people are concerned, they don't have much to do with us, though the respectable men are always glad to play poker with Pete."

She was honest, I thought, more honest than most women. I felt better now as long as I didn't move my head, so I gave her a closer look than I had before. Her eyes were blue, her hair very blonde, so light it was close to being silver. She was quite slender, but not too slender. As a matter of fact, she was very feminine.

Her features were regular, her lips full and red. They smiled easily, reflecting good humor that touched her eyes as well as her lips. She wore a blue, starched dress with a tight-fitting bodice, a dress that was perfect for her.

"What you're saying is that decent women don't have anything to do with you?"

She nodded, the quick smile touching her lips again. "That's right. They don't know I'm not married, they don't know that Pete took me out of a whorehouse four years ago, and that I've been traveling with him ever since. But it doesn't make any difference. They condemn me without knowing me, because I belong to a professional gambler."

"Women are tough on women," I said.

She had been sitting beside the bed. She rose, took the towel, wet it, wrung it out, and laid it back on my forehead. There was no smile on her lips then.

"You are terribly right," she said. "It has been my experience that the more decent they are, the harder they are on each other. I have only one female friend in town, a dressmaker named Sandra Lennon. You see, we both live in a kind of twilight area. We're not decent women, but we don't belong with the hookers, either."

"If she's a dressmaker," I said, "why is she living in this twilight area?"

The smile returned. "Because she makes dresses for the hookers. She's like me, you see. We're sort of in between."

Then she laughed out loud. "You know something, Mister Harmon? I think decent women hate men. Sandy and I are alike in that respect. We're men's women. We like men, and I guess we hate most women."

I shut my eyes. It didn't make any sense, but I knew what she meant. I hadn't had much to do with decent women since I'd left my grandmother's house, but I had learned quite a bit about them from her.

She always made a big to-do about being a decent woman, and I remembered how she and my grandfather talked about a businessman who had been gone from town for a week and had just got back. She had said he had a "bad disease."

I wouldn't forget what they'd said about a neighbor girl who had gotten pregnant. I hadn't run into this kind of attitude much during my drifting years because I hadn't had much contact with the solid, moral institutions that anchor our culture. I was surprised that Lucky was so conscious of it.

Presently she said: "I've got to go home and cook Pete's supper. I'll come back later." She reached over and took my hand that was nearest to her. "You'll be good while I'm gone?"

"Good?" I said. "Hell, I can't be anything else."

She squeezed my hand, and dropped it. "Then I won't worry," she said, and left the room.

I lay there, my eyes closed, thinking about Jeff Munro, then Pete Green, who had saved my life. At the moment I had no idea how those two men would affect my future. As the fellow says who writes books: "If I had only known. . . ." Then, for some reason, my thoughts turned to Sandra Lennon. I would like her, I told myself, and I was going to meet her before I left Miles City.

Chapter Three

At six o'clock I went downstairs to supper, but I couldn't eat. I drank a cup of coffee, then sat staring at the plate of food in front of me. I was sick to my stomach, and I knew that, if I did get anything down, it wouldn't stay long.

I went back upstairs, moving very slowly, and lay down again. The tick was filled with Montana "shavings"—that is, native hay—which at one time must have had a pleasant, fragrant smell, but that was long gone. It should have been changed months ago. Now the smell was most unpleasant, and the hay had gathered into lumps in some places and was entirely missing in others. To make it worse, the room was unbearably hot, but anything was better than being on my feet.

Lucky returned after dusk with Pete Green. She asked: "Have you been good?"

"I've been perfect," I said, "but I can't take any credit for my perfection."

Green had placed a bottle of whiskey on the bureau. Now he turned to the bed and stood, looking down at me. He was, I thought, typical of the professional gamblers who were drawn to mining camps and cow towns. He was tall and slender, with very long fingers. I had a notion he could do anything with a deck of cards that he wanted to.

He was a handsome man in a cool, detached sort of way. His eyes were pale blue, completely expressionless, as was his whole face, for that matter. Now, meeting his gaze, I couldn't tell anything about what he thought or felt.

"I hope you're on your feet soon," he said. "This town needs you."

"I'm not sure of that," I said. "I'm not sure I want to stay, either."

"Don't make a decision until you're feeling better," he said.

"Tell me something," I said. "You saved my life. Why?"

Again I felt he was a typical gambler. He smiled, but it told me nothing. Or maybe it wasn't really a smile; it was just a quick upturn of the lips that did not linger.

"Let's say I was establishing some credit," he said. "I figured you'd stay in Miles City. If you do, the time will come when you'll find a way to pay me back."

"I will if I stay," I said.

"You'll stay," he said, as if he had no doubt about it. "I'll have Lucky look in on you tomorrow. Maybe the whiskey will help you sleep."

Lucky leaned over me and kissed me, then she said: "Remember to be good."

"I'll remember," I said. "How can I forget?"

After they left, I lay there thinking about them. It was, I thought, a situation that would not last, but it would be Green's doing when and if it broke up. Lucky was a practical woman. Perhaps she loved Green, but regardless of that, almost anything was better than the whorehouse where he had found her. The break would come, I told myself, when the day came that she no longer brought him luck.

I wondered what Green had been before he turned gambler. I took him for a very intelligent man. He'd seen better days than this, I thought, or at least respectable days, somewhere in the Middle West or East. Probably something had happened that had driven him away from home. Maybe a dishonest business partner. Or a love affair that had gone bad. Or, to reverse my first guess, perhaps he had been the dishonest partner. Whatever it was, the chances were he would never go back, so he would continue gambling, and eventually someone would kill him.

The night was a long one, but the whiskey did help me sleep, although I woke a number of times before sunup. Sometime during the night a breeze sprang up that cooled the room, but it seemed that the bed got lumpier by the hour. Every time I woke up, I tried to find a more comfortable position. There wasn't one, I discovered, and, if I started to turn, my head began to ache.

When it was daylight, I went downstairs to the dining room and found I could eat. I had almost finished breakfast when Jeff Munro came in and joined me. His face was a mass of cuts and bruises, one eye was closed, and his nose was bandaged.

He took the chair across the table from me, asking: "How'd you sleep?"

"Not long at a time," I said. "And you?"

"The same. By God, Harmon, I hurt in a lot of places." The waitress came, and he gave his order, then added: "I had aimed to start up the Tongue today, but I guess I'll wait a day or two."

"Why did those plug uglies jump you?" I asked.

"You'd better ask why I wasn't ready for 'em when they did," he said angrily. "I knew some men were sitting at that back table, but I never gave 'em a second look, and that sure was a mistake. If I had seen who they were, I'd have called the marshal, but I stood there, talking to the bartender and then to you, and all the time they were waiting to give me a beating. They'd have beaten me to death if you hadn't jumped into the fracas."

"And Green," I said.

He nodded. "Yeah, and Green."

"You still haven't answered my question," I said.

24

"No, I guess I didn't," he said. "It was the night before I got to Miles City. I was riding with a cowboy who was headed for the Powder River country to take a job he'd been promised. We'd camped for the night beside the river at the edge of some willows. I left to take a look at our horses, when them three bastards moved in on the cowboy. If I'd been there, I guess they'd have got the drop on us and killed us and taken everything we had.

"I was just lucky that I was far enough away from the campfire so they didn't know I was there. I saw what was happening, so I eased up and got the drop on them. I took their guns and their boots, and marched 'em down the road. I told 'em that, if I ever saw 'em again, I'd kill 'em. I brought their horses in and turned 'em over to the sheriff, figuring that they were stolen. Their feet must be killing 'em, and I hope they are.

"Anyhow, my mistake was in figuring they wouldn't hang around here, but I guess they were waiting to square accounts with me. They had more guts than I allowed they'd have. It's been my experience that thieves are cowards, but I missed my guess with them."

"You said three?" I asked.

He nodded. "There were only three of 'em when they hit us. Who the fourth one was I don't know. He must have come in just to do what he did, kind of a reinforcement in case they got into trouble. It could be that the three of 'em were headed for Miles City to join up for some big robbery they'd planned. This is a purty tough town, and a lot of long riders go through here for one reason or another."

"Headed for the Black Hills, maybe," I suggested.

"Sure," Munro said. "It's been hell down there without the lid on. Trouble here is that it's a big county and the sheriff just don't have enough men to do the job. I don't think much of their court here, neither. A judge comes in from Helena, a political appointee who usually don't know Blackstone from the dictionary."

The waitress came with his breakfast, and he began to eat. I could see he had a better appetite than I had. I watched him for a time, and then I asked the question that had been prodding my mind for quite a while.

"Why did Pete Green give us a hand?" I asked.

He put his fork down and picked up his cup of coffee and took a drink, staring at me over the top of the cup. He put the cup down and said: "I thought maybe you knew. I don't, and that's a fact. I've played poker at his table some. I don't like him, but then I'm prejudiced against professional gamblers. I always figure they're too slick for me. I've won both nights I've played with him, so I guess he must be honest."

"He said he figured I'd stay here, and he was working up some credit," I said, "thinking that I'd find a way to repay him."

Munro nodded. "Might be. He's a cool customer. He wouldn't turn his hand to do anything if he didn't figure it was going to pay him one way or another."

"I had him pegged that way, too," I said, "but it strikes me he was playing a pretty long-odds bet. He had no reason to think I'd stay in Miles City."

Munro shook his head. "No, it strikes me it would have made a fair bet. Everybody knows you done a top-notch job in Clearwater and that Miles City needs a good lawman. They'll offer you the star. I'm surprised they haven't already."

"Hell, I don't know that I'll take it," I said. "I'm not even sure I want to be a lawman again."

"They'll give you a good salary," Munro said. "What else would you do? You want to cowboy? Work in a sawmill? Be a hide hunter? There's only going to be another year or two of that, anyhow."

I sat there, looking at Munro and thinking about it. I was also remembering what Munro had said about Miles City's being a good town, probably the biggest in eastern Montana. Sure, there was a risk in carrying a star, but there was a risk in just living in this country. The way Munro was jumped in Wolf's Saloon proved that. I wasn't convinced there was much more risk in being a lawman.

"I'll think about it," I said.

He pointed an index finger at me, and said: "You think hard. I want you to take the job. I've talked to some of the town fathers about you. That's why I know as much about it as I do."

"What's your interest in me taking the star?" I asked, thinking that he was being pretty damned pushy about it, and it irritated me.

"I'll tell you." He leaned forward. "It's like I said yesterday. Miles City will be the cattle and horse market of the country. I want it to have decent law enforcement, and it won't unless it's got a damned good marshal."

He leaned back and scratched his neck. "There's something else, though it's hard to make it sound like it makes any sense. I know what's going to happen in a few years with more people and more cattle and horses. This country's going to have an invasion of outlaws. Montana's big, and there's a lot of places to hide. It'll be a big thing, pushing cattle and horses over into Canada. I want to know there's somebody here who could give me a hand if I start crowding the outlaws. If it ain't me, it'll be somebody else who's better."

He convinced me. Like he said, it was hard to make it sound as if there was any sense to what he'd been saying, but he was in dead earnest. I had a crazy feeling, just sitting there

27

looking at him and listening to him, that he was taking a long look into the future. It was strange, and it scared me a little.

"I'll think about it," I said again. "I'll see you before you leave."

I got up and walked along both sides of Main Street. There was a good deal of activity going on, and I didn't have the impression Miles City was deserted as I'd had yesterday. A freight outfit was just pulling into town from somewhere, the Black Hills maybe. Men were standing in little knots along the street just talking. There were some women, too.

I heard the rumble of thunder. I glanced at the sky, clear and blue here, but black and menacing up the river. A storm was coming in, and the day would be cooler. Dust that was ankle-deep on Main Street would be a mud bath with a good rain.

My head was starting to pound, so I returned to my room, glad to get off my feet. Lucky came in about noon with a jar of vegetable soup she had made. She'd brought a bowl and a spoon and some crackers, so I moved my chair to the window and ate. She lay on the bed and watched me, smiling as if she found pleasure in seeing me eat. It was the first food I'd enjoyed since taking that crack on the head.

"You're a good cook, Lucky," I said.

"Thank you." She hesitated, then added in a low tone: "I'd make some man a good wife, wouldn't I?"

I nodded, thinking that was a strange thing for her to say. She tried to keep smiling, but suddenly I saw that she was close to tears. I realized, then, that her relationship with Pete Green was more tenuous than I had thought.

She didn't pursue it. In a few seconds she recovered her composure and, getting up from the bed, came to me and put a hand on my shoulder. "Are you going to settle down here?" she asked. "Are we making Miles City attractive enough?"

"I haven't decided," I said. "Where does your friend Sandra Lennon live?"

"She has a house on Sixth Street, south of Main. It's just before you come to the whorehouses. I told you she made dresses for the girls. That's why she bought the house she did. They don't come to Main Street, and she didn't want to go to their places." Lucky stopped and backed away. "Look at me, Dave Harmon. Are you falling in love with a woman before you even see her?"

I laughed. "Not exactly. I just wanted to look at her."

"She's good to look at," Lucky said. "We got off the subject. You'll take the star when it's offered, won't you? Pete and I would be very unhappy if you turned it down."

"I wouldn't want that to happen," I said. "You think that really was the reason he saved my life yesterday?"

"Of course," she said. "He's an honest man. He wouldn't lie to you. Naturally it's to his interest to have a man carrying the star who is his friend. It's all the better if he owes Pete his life."

"Then I'll have to take the star, won't I?"

"Certainly," she said and, leaning down, kissed me. "I'll come in tomorrow."

"I'll be all right by then," I said.

"I hope so," she said, and left the room.

I resented the pressure that was being put on me to take a job I hadn't even been offered, although I could understand it. They had heard about my work in Clearwater, and I knew that a good lawman was hard to find. I considered myself a good one, and I was certain I'd get better with experience. Still, I resented pressure, and I told myself I was going to make up my own mind.

I thought about Lucky for a while. She was in love with Pete Green, but she wasn't sure of him. I had a feeling she would do anything for him, that she'd go to bed with me if it would persuade me to take the marshal's job. I'll admit the situation interested me, but I was never one to take another man's woman. Besides, I still wanted to see Sandra Lennon before I made a decision about staying in Miles City.

Chapter Four

The next morning I was sitting in Wolf's Saloon after seeing Munro and a couple other men leave town for their trip up the Tongue River when the offer came. Pete Green and Lucky hadn't showed up yet. The place was empty except for the bartender and a couple of cowboys who were drinking at the bar.

I had talked to them briefly, but I didn't feel like standing up any longer, so I took my drink and sat down at a table near a window. About ten minutes later three men came in, saw me, and came directly to my table.

The first man was the doctor. My memory of him was pretty vague, but I recognized him. I hadn't seen the other two before. One was a tall, skinny man with an Adam's apple that bobbed around uncertainly as he talked. The third was short, about as tall as the doctor, and fat. He was sweating and kept mopping his face with a bandanna. His cheeks were pink and he was puffing when he came into the saloon, as if he had been running, but neither of the others was even breathing hard.

The doctor introduced himself first. "I'm Doc Lewis," he said. "We've met, but very briefly, and you may not have heard my name. We have an advantage in the respect that everybody in town knows you."

He held out his hand, and I shook it. He motioned to the skinny man. "This is Joe Abbot. He owns the Mercantile." I shook his hand, not sure whether I liked him or not. His grip was firm enough, but there was a kind of slick-fish feeling about his hand. It wasn't anything to condemn a man about, so I reserved judgment.

Doc Lewis motioned to the fat man. "Abe Calder. He owns the jewelry store on Main, between Sixth and Seventh Streets."

I liked Abe Calder. His grip was firm, he looked me squarely in the eyes when he shook hands with me, and I had a strong feeling he was a man who could be depended on. Funny about first impressions. I usually find them reliable when they hit me immediately with a kind of certainty about them, which this one did. On the other hand, I have to wait a while to make up my mind when a man strikes me the way Abbot did. The chances were I'd neither like nor trust a man like that, although I have made mistakes in judgment. It's just a matter of not being real sure about them at first.

They sat down at my table, Doc Lewis motioning to the bartender to bring a bottle and glasses. He filled the glasses as soon as they came, and looked at me. I shook my head. I was never one to drink very much in the morning. Besides, most of my drink was still in the glass.

"We're representing Miles City," Lewis said. "I'm sure you know why we're here. Jeff Munro said he had talked to you. Actually the idea of hiring you as town marshal occurred to us before Jeff mentioned it. We're all of the same mind. We don't want our town to become another Dodge City. It could very well have the same bloody reputation, if we let things get out of hand."

Abbot leaned forward. He looked at me, yet he wasn't looking at me. His gaze seemed fixed on a spot just above my head. "Harmon, I had the first store in town," he said. "I came here because I had confidence in this location for a city. In the past two or three years since Milestown was started, we've had certain problems that have held back its growth. Transportation for one thing. The only method we've had to get bulky material here is the riverboat, but they can't come except during high water from May to September. That's a short time. Sometimes it's even less in the low water years. Otherwise, we have freight trains and stagecoaches, but it's a long, hard trip from Bismarck. Now we'll have the Northern Pacific building into Miles City within a year. That takes care of the transportation problem."

He picked up his drink and gulped it, then he went on. "Another problem is the buffalo, but they'll be gone in a year or two, and the range will be open for cattle. We'll have 'em, too, by God, millions of 'em. Most of the herds coming up from Texas will drive down the Tongue, and they'll bring business to Miles City. The third problem was the Indians, and they've pretty well been taken care of. The fact that the fort is close is one reason we haven't had any Indian trouble, and we wont have it in the future. Sure, we'll have Indians camped along the Tongue River or the Yellowstone, but they'll walk mighty easy with the troops two miles away."

Abe Calder had been watching me, his eyes half closed, as if studying me and making a judgment about me. Now he picked up the conversation. "We're not fixing to sell you any real estate, Harmon. Whether you invest in property is up to you. We have invested heavily, and we expect to make some money out of our investment. For that reason we can't afford to let Miles City become a bloody ground and get a lawless reputation. That's why we want your services."

Doc Lewis nodded. "Some of the toughs you ran out of Clearwater stopped here. Several of them overstayed their welcome. Anyhow, we heard about you through them. They didn't have much good to say about you except that you are a tough son-of-a-bitch."

"However," Abbot said, "there are degrees of toughness. We don't want a man who's a killer, and that's a very common fault among marshals who get the reputation of being town tamers. I guess we want a man who goes down the middle. He won't kill just for the pleasure of killing, as some men do. On the other hand, he'll kill a man if he has to."

Both Calder and Lewis nodded agreement. Lewis said: "We wanted to say this before we made you a firm offer. You don't know much about us, so maybe you want to ask some questions before we get down to cases."

"I do," I said. "You've got a marshal. Why are you looking for another man?"

"We'll keep the man we've got," the doctor said. "His name is Bill Dillon. He's not the best man in the world, and he knows it, but he'll stay on if we get another marshal to split the day. He prefers the midnight-to-noon shift. You would take the noon-to-midnight. Each man is obligated to help the other one in case of an emergency. You'll be the chief, and you'd give the orders. You would also receive more pay."

I had no complaint about that arrangement. I said: "How does the town look on the soldiers?"

"As a damned nuisance," Abbot said sharply, and this time his gaze met mine. "By God, I wish we didn't have a soldier within a hundred miles. I'll admit they have protected us from the Indians. We do a lot of business with the post, and the soldiers spend most of their pay here in town, so we can't get along without them."

Calder nodded. "I'll tell you something, Harmon, though you had soldiers at Clearwater and I guess they are all about alike. Generally speaking, they are a pretty low class of men. Some are running from the law, and the Army is a good place to hide. Some are failures at everything they've tried, so they enlist just to get three meals a day. Some are foreigners who can't get work. They'd been in a European army, so they just naturally gravitated into the U.S. Army when they got to this country."

34

"You're not answering the question I asked," I said. "Suppose a couple of soldiers get into a fight. What's the town's attitude? In other words, what does it expect from its marshal?"

"This has been a pretty tough town," Doc Lewis said slowly. "We might just as well admit it. We've had out share of badmen. We've let them settle their own problems. Same with the soldiers. On pay day they make a rush for the Cottage Saloon. That's their favorite hang-out. Maybe they'll go to a whorehouse. By midnight they're probably broke. If they have a fight, let them fight. If you go in there when a crowd of them are in the saloon, you'll have more than you can handle. I'd say the only time when you would be obliged to interfere is when a town man gets into trouble. The swaddies stick together, which is to be expected."

"We let the Army discipline its own," Calder said, "although we realize it can't always do it."

I nodded. "Fair enough. Now, this question is a tough one, but it's important for a lawman to have answered. In a town like this, the wealthier men are likely to invest in saloons and whorehouses along with their regular businesses. The respectable men are likely to do business in the whorehouse. Now, where does that leave the marshal? Does he look the other way in cases where your town interest conflicts with the law?"

They were silent for a few seconds, all three looking as guilty as hell. Then Lewis laughed. "You're a forthright man, Harmon. I like that. I guess we wouldn't want it any other way. What you're saying is that you aim to be your own boss in such a situation and not have the townsmen dictating what you do."

"That's right," I said. "If my hands are to be tied, and I'm not allowed to enforce the law as I see it, I don't want the job. There are times when you have to close a place. I'll do it if I think it's necessary, or you'll find another marshal."

"I think that's fair," Abbot said. "You hit hard, Harmon. I own one of the whorehouses. I could be putting my tail in a crack, but I think you've got to have a free hand."

Calder nodded. "Agreed."

Doc Lewis nodded his agreement. "Suppose something happens that turns the town against you? What would you do?"

"I won't be hard to get rid of if that's what you mean," I said.

"That's what I meant," Lewis said. "I expect the general climate around here to improve in another year or two. The hide hunters are like the soldiers. We don't like them, but they bring business, so we put up with them. In another year or two, they'll be gone."

"Maybe not," I said. "They may find something else to do. Chopping wood for the riverboats. They might even end up as wolfers."

"These things are all going to pass," Lewis said a little impatiently. "The railroad will bring women, and women always tame frontier towns. I don't think we'll have these problems in two, three years."

Calder picked up his glass, stared at it, then set it back on the table. "I don't know about that, Doc. Sure, we'll grow up, but it may take more time than you're giving it."

"We'll be getting a better quality of women in our whorehouses," Abbot said. "The cowboys will demand it. They say that a whore goes to the dogs, then she goes to the soldiers. The hide hunters are a notch lower. This situation has to improve."

"Are you trying to tell me that the quality of whores has anything to do with the quality of the town?" Calder demanded.

"In a way, yes," Abbot said. "Cowboys are a pretty decent lot. I wouldn't say it's the whores who elevate the town. It's the men themselves. The wives, too, and we'll be getting more wives."

"I might question that," the doctor said. "I'm not sure the wives will improve the town. They might try to purify it, and we won't stand for that."

"One more thing," I said. "Suppose we have big trouble . . . more than two of us can handle. How much support can I expect from the town?"

"As much as you need," Abbot said. "All you have to do is to holler."

The answer came too quickly, I thought. It was a question they had expected, and there was only one answer they could give. I didn't say so, but I didn't believe Abbot.

"Well," Lewis said, "you interested?"

"Yes, I'm interested," I said.

"All right," Doc Lewis said. "We'll pay you one hundred dollars a month. Is that satisfactory?"

It was more than I had expected. I didn't know of any other kind of work that would pay me as much. I knew then I would take it, but I didn't want to say so yet.

"Let me think about it for a day or so," I said. "I'm not skookum enough yet to start right now."

"Twenty-four hours," he said. "If you don't want the job, we'll have to send away for a man. We can't afford to wait much longer."

"That's right," Abbot agreed. "The hide hunters will be drifting in before long, and we'll have a deluge of cowboys when the herds get here."

"Twenty-four hours," Lewis repeated.

They left. I felt vaguely let down. I'm not sure why, except that I sensed they expected me to accept on the spot, and they were a little huffy that I hadn't.

"Well," Pete Green said, "how about it? Are you going to accept their offer?"

I turned around. Green and Lucky had arrived and were sitting at the next table. Lucky was smiling, as if she had no doubt what I would say.

"I'm thinking it over," I said. "I haven't seen Sandra Lennon yet."

"What's that got to do with it?" Green asked.

"He's in love with her, just from what I've told him about her," Lucky said. "He wants to see her."

"Well, take him over and introduce him," Green said.

"Not today," I said. "I'm going back to my room."

"I'd better tell you one thing," Green said. "If you take the job and if you get into more than you can handle, you will get no help from the ribbon clerks you were talking to. Help will come from men like me."

"I believe that," I said.

I left the saloon and walked out into the hot morning. The thunderstorm of the night before had been more sound than rain. The shower had been a light one. I turned toward the hotel. I couldn't keep from thinking about what Green had said. The more help he gave me, the more favors he would expect. I didn't like it, not one damned bit.

Chapter Five

Lucky came in about noon with another bowl of soup. I said: "You don't need to feed me after today. I'm all right."

She smiled and shook her head. "Think you could put up a good fight today?"

"I'm not fighting anybody," I said. "Not today."

"You didn't answer my question," she said.

"Well, no, not if I took on a tough man."

"There are plenty of tough men in Miles City," she said gravely, "and you'll have to fight some of them about the time you pin on your star. Now get up into a chair and eat my offering. I won't come any more if I bother you."

I obeyed, glancing at her as I wondered what kind of a life she had led since she'd thrown in with Green. Finally I asked her.

She sat on the edge of the bed and stared at me for a full minute. Finally she said: "I'm thankful to have a bed to sleep in and three meals a day and nice dresses to wear. If that was all there is to life, I would have a perfect situation."

"What else is there?" I asked.

"You wouldn't understand," she said, "so I won't attempt to tell you."

"Try me," I said.

She rose, and walked to the window. A freight outfit bound for Fort Keogh had just pulled into town, and I could hear varieties of racket from the street. She didn't say a word until I had finished the soup, then she turned to face me.

"A woman never sees life the way a man does," she said with a hint of bitterness. "I guess I love Pete. He's done a lot for me. I've told you that. At first we knocked around from one town to another. He never seemed to get ahead much, and there were days when we didn't have enough to eat or a decent place to sleep. He was broke half a dozen times. I guess I worried. I began to wonder if I'd helped myself any by going off with him.

"We drifted up into the Black Hills, and, one night in Deadwood, Pete hit the jackpot. He cleaned out one of the big mining men. He said afterward it was the biggest run of luck he'd ever had. The last hand he played that night won ten thousand dollars for him. The next morning we left for Miles City. He was afraid the mining man would hire some plug uglies to take the money away from him.

"Since we've been here, he's been up and down. He's never been broke, but he hasn't made any big money, either. I don't worry any more about not getting my three meals a day or a decent bed to sleep in. Pete always comes up with something."

She wiped her face with a handkerchief. "I guess it's security I want, and don't have. I mean, the kind of security that a husband gives. It's children and a house you own and the recognition of the decent women in town. It's the feeling that your man will stay with you until the day one of you dies."

She threw up her hands. "Oh, I don't know, Dave. Sometimes I think I should never have a thought past today. Nobody knows what tomorrow will bring anyhow, even the most secure of women, but I can't get over living in this twilight zone I told you about the other day. I guess that's what bothers me."

"I think I savvy that," I said, "but it's my guess that what bothers you even more is the fear that one day Pete will say you're not bringing him luck any more, so he's throwing you out."

"Yes, that's right," she said in a low voice. "I don't know that Pete loves me. I sometimes wonder if he even knows what love is. He likes to have me in bed with him. Maybe that's all he wants. I live day by day, and I don't know if I'll have to go back into a whorehouse tomorrow or not."

"You could go to work," I said.

"At what?" she asked scornfully. "Maybe keeping house for a man like Joe Abbot and having to fight every night to keep him out of my bed? No, if I have to live that way, I might just as well go into a whorehouse. Not here, though. They've got the worst batch of cows I ever saw. You won't believe it. Hide hunters and soldiers don't demand much. Just two legs with a hole between them."

I knew that, if I asked her to move in with me, she'd do it. I wasn't sure she was telling me the whole truth. I had a hunch that she was getting tired of Green, but she'd hang onto him until a better man came along.

Maybe I was conceited and doing a little self-bragging, but I was convinced that she thought I was a better man. Even so, I had no intention of having to fight Green for a woman I didn't particularly want.

"You don't need to worry about bothering me," I said. "I just don't want to make Pete jealous."

She snorted derisively. "One thing you won't make him is jealous."

"Tell me about your friend Sandra," I said.

"Why?"

"I just want to know about her."

Lucky chewed on her lower lip a moment, then she said thoughtfully: "This is the damnedest thing I ever heard of. I just mentioned her, and you start making dreams about her. Why?"

"Oh, I don't know," I said. "Curious, I guess."

"She makes beautiful hats and dresses," Lucky said. "She's not pretty, but she's attractive. She's not the thin-lipped, pious kind of woman who delights in being a good wife, but she couldn't live in a whorehouse, either. I really don't know much about her, Dave. I've visited with Sandy ever since I've been in Miles City, but there's a lot of mystery about her. She's never told me much about her life, except that she was living in an Idaho mining camp before she came here."

"Mystery adds to a woman's attractiveness," I said.

"Maybe so," Lucky said. "To a man, that is. To a woman she's just plain stubborn, and that makes her frustrating."

"I'm going to see her this afternoon," I said.

"Don't do it!" she cried. "Not until I can go with you and introduce you all fit and proper."

"Is she that kind of a woman?"

"Not exactly, but it would help you get off on the right foot."

"I'll take my chances," I said.

She flushed angrily. "All right, but don't blame me if she throws you out."

She picked up the soup bowl and stomped out of the room. I lay down for a while, mopping my face with my bandanna. I didn't think the temperature was as high as it had been the day before, but the storm had left a muggy feeling in the air that made the heat feel worse. Outside, the noise had quieted down. Once in a while I'd hear a rider trot his horse down Main Street, or I'd hear the gentle swish of a buggy's wheels in the deep dust of the street.

I wondered how much of Lucky's anger was over my insistence on seeing Sandra alone, or if it was aroused by her desire to hold me for herself with the hope that I would take her from Green. Like every other woman I had ever known fairly well, Lucky was fickle and selfish, and the knowledge made me think less of her.

In the middle of the afternoon I rose, washed, and combed my hair, and left the hotel. I walked slowly along the street, feeling better than I had, maybe because I was excited over the prospect of seeing Sandra Lennon.

I'll grant that this whole thing was ridiculous, but the fact remained that I had made some dreams about her, just as Lucky had said. Although I wasn't sure what I expected when I saw her, I did know I expected to see something unusual and something good.

I made the turn to the right on Sixth Street and came to her house, which faced on Sixth. On beyond were several large buildings, which I assumed were the whorehouses. Sandra's house had a white picket fence along the street. I opened the gate and went into the yard. It had grown up in weeds, which had been cut, so it was not the jungle that most front yards in Miles City were.

The house was a log one with a false front, so I guessed it had been built for use as some kind of a store. I stepped up on the porch and knocked, but there was no answer. On the door were the words in black letters **SANDRA LENNON,** and below, in smaller letters, **MILLINER AND DRESS-MAKER.**

I assumed the front room at least was public, so I opened the door and stepped inside. I called—"Miss Lennon?"—but there was no answer. I glanced around at the cutting table, the dressmaker's dummy, the box filled with an assortment of thread, needles, and thimbles, the two rawhide-bottom chairs, and the rocker, thinking this was exactly what I would expect. Several shelves on one wall held a number of bolts of bright-colored cloth. A partly finished blue velvet dress was draped over the back of one of the chairs.

43

She wasn't in the house, I decided, so I left the room, closing the front door, and then, prompted by some vague impulse, I walked around the house to the back. She was there, down on her hands and knees in her garden, weeding a row of carrots. She had a good vegetable garden of potatoes, beets, cabbage, and carrots. The only flowers she had were a row of hollyhocks along the back fence.

I said: "Miss Lennon?"

She jumped, startled, and turned her head to look at me. She was a damned fine-looking woman. That was my first general impression. She got up, frowning, and I saw that she was a little plumper than I had expected, but not too much so.

Her hair was black, pulled back from her forehead and tied with a red ribbon back of her neck. Her lips were full and expressive. Her face was quite tanned, so I assumed she spent a good deal of her time in her garden.

For a good part of a minute she stood, motionless, staring at me as if trying to place me. Finally she asked: "Who are you and what do you want?"

"I hope I haven't intruded . . . ," I began.

"I asked you who you were and what you wanted." Her voice was sharper this time.

Suddenly I was afraid. She was everything I had hoped for. I took a long breath, knowing that I liked what I saw and I wanted her. I hoped I hadn't ruined my chances, and I wished, now that it was too late, that I had waited until Lucky could come with me. Bur right now, how was I going to tell her what I wanted?

I said lamely: "I'm Dave Harmon. I just wanted to meet you. I knocked on your door, but. . . ."

"Dave Harmon," she said. "Lucky mentioned you to me. You're the Clearwater marshal, aren't you?"

The gathering anger had left her. Now she walked toward

me, being careful not to step on the carrots. It didn't make any difference to me that she was wearing an old dress that was soiled where she had been on her knees and that she had a streak of dirt along one cheek. Nothing made any difference. She had an animated, expressive face. She was beautiful. I would never find another woman like her.

"I was the Clearwater marshal," I said. "I'm going to be the Miles City marshal."

"Good," she said. "We need a good marshal in Miles City. I understand you did a good job in Clearwater."

"I didn't come here to talk about that," I said. "Miss Lennon, I. . . ."

"I'm not Miss Lennon," she said. "I'm Sandy to my friends."

"Then you're Sandy to me," I said. "I came to tell you that I'm going to marry you and, if there are any other men interested in you, tell them to get out of the way, because I'll simply run over them if they don't."

She stared at me blankly, her eyes wide, her lips parted. She said: "Mister Harmon, you must be completely mad."

"My friends call me Dave," I said. "You are right. I am absolutely and completely mad. Forgive me for coming unannounced, but I wanted to see you. I'll be back tomorrow."

I turned and walked away, leaving her staring at me with the same blank, unbelieving expression. All I could do was to hope she wasn't offended. As far as I was concerned, I had never been more serious in my life, although this had been the last thing I had intended to do.

On the way back to the hotel, I stopped at the Mercantile and told Joe Abbot that I would take the job, starting at noon the next day.

Chapter Six

I was able to rent a small cabin near the jail and marshal's office. A shed behind it gave adequate shelter for my horse. I furnished it with a bed, a cook stove, a table, and two chairs. I bought enough dishes and groceries to get started, and moved in, glad to escape from the hotel, where the food was almost as bad as the bed. I wasn't the best cook in the world, but I preferred my cooking to the hotel's.

The following noon I showed up at the jail. Bill Dillon was sitting in the swivel chair, his feet cocked on the desk. He said: "It's time I was turning this town over to you, and it gives me pleasure to do it."

I took a good look at him. I'd seen him that day in Wolf's Saloon, but I didn't remember much of what I'd seen. He was about forty, I judged, tall and slim, bald-headed, with a heavy, downthrusting mustache.

For some reason I had a feeling that Bill Dillon was a lightweight, but again it was that first impression, which on occasion was wrong, although I had learned to respect it because it was right more times than it was wrong.

I shook hands with him, asking: "Now, why does it give you pleasure to turn the town over to me?"

"You're the head man," he said. "You get the fat salary, you get the responsibility, and you'll get the kicks. I've been getting 'em, and I've had enough. Trying to satisfy a man like Joe Abbot is hell on high red wheels. I'll be glad to take less money and let you try to give 'em what they want."

I walked around the office. It was little different from other lawmen's offices I had been in, with a gun rack on one

46

wall filled with several rifles, a battered desk and an equally battered swivel chair, and a couple of rawhide-bottomed chairs. Several Reward dodgers were tacked to the wall near the door. A potbellied stove was in one corner of the room, a spittoon on the floor beside it.

I swung around to face Dillon. "What's so tough about satisfying Abbot?"

"He is two-faced," Dillon said. "You can tell him I said so if you want to. If he fires me, he'll be doing me a favor. He's like a lot of businessmen. He's got his feet on both sides of the fence. He owns the store, and, therefore, he's a legitimate businessman, but he also owns the Golden Palace, the first whorehouse you come to on Sixth Street after you leave Main. He'll beat hell out of one of his girls, but, by God, you'd better not interfere."

I wasn't surprised. I'd run into situations like this before. When I'd mentioned it in Wolf's Saloon where the three men had offered me the job, I had sensed this very thing. Abbot had almost admitted it in saying he owned one of the whorehouses. The point was that, if a marshal made his position clear when he started, he wouldn't get run over. Apparently Dillon had not done this.

"I'll handle him," I said. "I'll have to."

"You sure as hell will, because I can't." Dillon rose, and started toward the door, then he stopped and said: "We've had some tough nuts here, like Calamity Jane and Big Nose George Parrot. X. Biedler shows up once in a while if he thinks a wanted man is holed up here, and he expects help when he picks up his man. The sheriff has a hell of a big county, and he ain't got the men to do the job. The town's all ours."

I nodded, expecting that. As far as the tough nuts went, I figured any town that had the frontier growing pains Miles

City did would draw its share. I said: "You've got something else on your mind that you want to say, Dillon. Now, let's hear it, if it's anything I need to know."

"You need to know, all right," Dillon said slowly, "but I guess it comes under the head of gossip, because I can't prove it. Everybody in town thinks it, but mostly they're afraid to say it out loud. It's my opinion that Joe Abbot is the head of the toughs, while all the time he's pretending to be a town father and a legitimate businessman. He owns a ranch down the river about a mile, and he always keeps a big bunch of horses on hand. I think he deals with all the outlaws who come through here, trading horses and furnishing 'em with grub. He don't do any real ranching. He's in the horse business."

"The sheriff can't touch him?"

Dillon shook his head. "He's been out there a dozen times in the last year, but he never finds a wanted man hiding out with Abbot, and he's never proved any of the horses in Abbot's corral are stolen. Maybe he goes the wrong time. All I know is that nobody has ever laid a hand on Joe Abbot."

I walked to the metal door that led into the jail. I opened it, and stepped inside. There was just one big room, and it was empty. I stepped back into the office, asking: "What happened to the three men who beat Munro up?"

"I turned 'em loose yesterday and told 'em to get out of town and stay out," Dillon said. "If I'd known you were taking the job of head man, I'd have waited and let you turn 'em loose."

"If it had been me," I said sharply, "they'd still be here. They should have stood trial for attempted murder."

He nodded and smiled. "You are right, Harmon. You are absolutely right. It's just that you haven't met Joe Abbot. I mean, not since you pinned on the star."

I didn't press him, but I did have one more question. "What about Doc Lewis and Abe Calder and the rest of the businessmen?"

"As far as I know," Dillon said, "they're all straight. At least they've never interfered with me, but they're afraid of Abbot, too. I can promise you one thing. You won't get any backing from them if Abbot don't want to give it."

I remembered what Pete Green had said, that if I got any help, it would be from men like him, not the ribbons clerks I'd been talking to. I suddenly had a feeling that there was more truth to what he'd said than I had thought, and I believed him when I heard it.

"I don't savvy," I said. "Why did Abbot hire me? He came to see me with Calder and Doc Lewis. He could have blocked it. Maybe he wasn't as anxious for me to take the job as the other two were, but he didn't make it tough for me, either."

Dillon nodded. "I wondered about that. I think there were three reasons. Jeff Munro was pushing for you, and he's a big man in the territory. Abbot didn't want to buck him. Number two, Abbot always appears to be on the side of the law, and people believe he is because of his business. As far as I know, his store has always been honest. Number three, Abbot is the kind of man who thinks so much of himself that he always figures he can outsmart the other fellow, so he's not afraid of you."

Dillon was making sense, and my respect for him grew. I had a feeling that back somewhere along the way he'd been chopped down to size by Abbot and was staying on as marshal in the hopes he would see me chop Abbot down.

"Bill," I said, "I think we can handle him, but we've got to know who will side with us if it comes to a showdown between the two factions."

"It's gonna come," Dillon said gravely, "but you never

know who's on your side till the blue chip's finally down. I've got a hunch that some of the saloon owners and gamblers who don't belong to the *decent* crowd will be the ones who'll side us."

I nodded agreement, thinking again of Pete Green. "We'll see," I said, "though I'd like to know who they are before the showdown comes."

"I'm going home, and I'm going to bed," Dillon said. "It's gonna be good to be on a twelve-hour shift instead of a twenty-four-hour one. Don't be misled by the town being quiet right now. It'll be popping at the seams before long."

"What about the soldiers?"

"The swaddies?" Dillon shrugged. "They don't bother the townspeople much, so we let 'em alone most of the time. They'll fight amongst themselves. If it gets too bad, notify the fort. They'll take care of it."

He left then. I stood in the doorway and watched him stride down Main Street, then turn off on Fifth. I felt better about him, though. I didn't like the idea of getting into what looked like a personal feud between him and Joe Abbot.

I set out to get acquainted with the businessmen of Miles City, working my way along one side of Main Street, then back along the other. I stopped in every store, saloon, shop, and office, and shook hands with the proprietors. By actual count there were twenty-three saloons. Someone said there was a church, but I didn't get it spotted that afternoon.

If it was a store or office, I simply said who I was and that I would be on duty between noon and midnight, and to let me know if there was anything I could do for them. I was tougher on the saloonkeepers, because trouble in a town like Miles City starts usually in a whorehouse or a saloon. I said that, if I found out that any of them doped a drink and robbed a man, I'd close the place. If there was any resistance, I'd jail the owner.

One man named Fred Holmes who had a small saloon on Main between Sixth and Seventh got proddy about it and said nobody was going to close him down.

"If you don't roll any of your customers," I said, "you don't need to worry."

"I don't let my customers get rolled," he snapped, "but I ain't standing still and letting you come around here the first day you pin on your star and talk about closing me down."

"If you run an honest place," I said, "you'll stand still for it, all right."

He began to swell up like a pigeon. "The hell I will!" he yelled. "By God, I'll kill me a smart-aleck marshal before I let him close my place of business down."

"Let's not put anything off," I said. "I told you what I'd do. Now, you go ahead and kill me."

Some of the steam went out of him. He said sullenly: "I can wait."

I left the saloon, telling myself that, if he ever sent for help, I might have some things to do before I got to him. At that I felt fortunate, because he was the only sour apple I hit all afternoon. Most of the businessmen said they were glad to have me in Miles City, that there had been too much lawlessness in town, and they'd co-operate in every way they could.

I purposely bypassed Wolf's Saloon until I had gone to all the others, then I went in and made my spiel to the bartender who owned the place. Green's table was vacant except for Green, who sat there idly shuffling a deck of cards. I bought a drink and sat down across from him.

"Glad you got started, Dave," Green said. "The last time I saw you I thought you looked a little puny."

"I was," I said. "I still am. I hope we don't have an epidemic of crime."

"You won't for a while," he said, "but it's the calm before

the storm. It'll come in a few weeks. Maybe not crime, but a lot of damned monkey business."

I leaned forward. I said: "Pete, what kind of a marshal is Bill Dillon?"

"Good," he said. "It's just that he didn't have as much gumption as he should have. He never looked too hard or too long for a man he wanted, and he'll knuckle down if you run over him roughshod, but for what we wanted, he's been all right."

"Are you telling me that nobody's wanted a tight town?"

"You could put it that way," Green said, "though you'll never get anyone to admit it. It's all a matter of good business. They pretty well told you that, the morning they hired you."

"And if I step on too many toes?"

He grinned that quick upturn at the corners of his mouth. "Don't step on any toes. They hired you, and they can fire you."

"Particularly Joe Abbot?"

"Been hearing a little gossip?"

"A little."

"Don't believe all you hear," Green said, "and don't set out to bust Abbot. Nobody bucks him."

I thought about it as I walked to my cabin and started supper. The first day wearing the star had been an eye-opener. I was never one to put important things off. If Joe Abbot was the big cheese hereabouts, and if he worked with the tough element, then it was time I was finding out. If I got fired, then I'd better get that done, too.

Chapter Seven

I visited the whorehouses as soon as I finished supper, starting with Abbot's Golden Palace. Joe Abbot wasn't there. I hadn't expected him to be. It had been my experience that in a situation like this the owner was always away unless he visited the house for his own pleasure, or the take was down from the past average and he suspected some hanky-panky on the part of the madam. As a matter of fact, I was glad he wasn't there. I didn't want any kind of a showdown yet. I figured it would come soon enough.

The madam was big-boned, big-breasted, and big-hipped. Her name was Maggie Adams. She ushered me into the parlor and motioned me to sit down. I glanced around, amazed by the opulence of the place. I hadn't expected so much luxury in a town like Miles City.

There were two sofas, three rocking chairs, a piano, several pictures on the wall, which was covered by red-flowered wallpaper, and a claw-footed maple stand in the center of the room. A hobnailed lamp was on the top of the stand, along with three or four books and a magazine or two.

Maggie apparently sensed my amazement. She smiled as she said: "You have a right to be surprised, marshal. This is the nicest place between Bismarck and the coast cities. As a matter of fact, I doubt that you will find anything as luxurious in Bismarck. Or Deadwood."

"It is nice," I said.

"Our girls are of the same quality. We are purposely too high-priced for hide hunters and soldiers." She pointed to a sign near the hall door that read **WE CHOOSE OUR CUSTOMERS.** She said: "We mean that. We turn away drunks. A man who is filthy dirty. A man we know is a troublemaker. In fact, we don't want any men that we don't think are fit for the girls. We cater to cowboys, Army officers, and businessmen."

"Then I guess you don't have any problems," I said.

She had freckles, red hair, and the kind of happy, Irish face that smiled most of the time. Now there was no trace of a smile on her lips as she studied me for several seconds. "Marshal," she said, "we do have a problem, and I don't know what to do about it."

She was sitting in a rocking chair. I was across from her on a black leather sofa. Now she rose and crossed the room and sat down beside me.

"Yes, Marshal," she said, "we have a problem, and I say I'm damned if I know what to do about it."

"Anything I can do?"

"You sure can," she answered. "I'm a good judge of men. I have to be. I ain't afraid to weed 'em out. I've been in this business for a long time. I've dealt with all kinds of men from here to Chicago. I've slept with 'em. I've learned what they like, and I train my girls to please them, but, by God, I draw the line at some things. Beating a girl is one of 'em."

"That's the kind of man you ought to weed out first thing," I said.

"I know," she said bitterly, "but I can't weed him out. He owns the place."

"Joe Abbot?"

She nodded. "Joe Abbot."

"I'll be damned."

This was something I hadn't heard about Abbot, except for what Dillon had said, and I hadn't believed that, figuring that Dillon was sore at Abbot and he'd made it up. I scratched the back of my neck and looked at Maggie, who was watching me as if measuring me right there on the spot.

"I've heard about your work in Clearwater," she said. "They tell me you're on the square. That's the way I size you up. I wouldn't be telling you this if I didn't think you could be trusted. Bill Dillon was afraid of Joe, so he wouldn't do anything. I've done all I could, telling Joe I'd kill him if he does it again. He laughs at me and says I've got a good job, and, if I don't want it, he can find a woman to replace me anytime I decide to quit. He figures I won't kill him, but, by God, I just might fool him."

She hitched a little closer to me. "Marshal, he does it only to new girls. He says it's his right to try 'em out, and beating is part of his . . . well, he calls it *testing*. If they don't suit him, he says they won't suit other men." She opened her hands in a gesture of futility. "What do I do?"

"Call me," I said. "Let me know the next time you got a new girl."

"You're not afraid of Joe?"

"No. Should I be?"

"He's got a lot of power," she said evasively. "I take care of my girls, Marshal. I've never had a suicide, and I very seldom have one quit."

"You let me know," I said. "Do you have a house man?"

"Yes. He's big and strong, and he does a good job, except for Joe Abbot. Joe hired him, not me, so he wouldn't do anything to the man who pays his wages."

"Call me the next time it happens," I said. "Now, then, I want to see your girls."

She was surprised at that, but she didn't argue. In about five minutes she had them lined up in front of me, six of them. They were surprisingly good-looking girls, most of them young, and all of them the kind of women you'd expect to see on Miles City's Main Street.

Maggie introduced them by name. Then I said: "I'm Dave Harmon. I'll be working with Bill Dillon from now on. I have the noon-to-midnight shift. I want to tell you two things. First, I will not stand for any lawbreaking on your part. If I hear of you rolling a man, I'll close this place and I'll jail the woman who did it."

"Marshal," Maggie cried, "that never happens here!"

One girl named Rosebud looked like the pert kind of girl who felt no reverence for anyone. She said coolly: "Marshal, you are a liar. You wouldn't lock one of us up with the kind of men who populate your jail. I happen to know that there is only one room in your jail."

"Try me," I said.

Rosebud laughed and flipped her hips in what she considered a titillating manner. "No, Marshal, I wouldn't roll a man just to try you, but I still think you're lying about it and trying to scare us. You'd better come here and try me."

"I'm trying to scare you, all right," I said. "I don't want trouble, but I'm not lying. Now, the second thing I want to tell you is that anytime you need me, send for me."

"Thank you, Marshal," Maggie said.

"Come back and see me," Rosebud said, still laughing softly, as if she thought she had challenged me and won a victory.

I put on my hat and walked out, tempted to take Rosebud up on her invitation.

I visited all of the houses by dark. Pete Green was right. The other places were barns, the women a sorry lot. I could believe that Maggie Adams got the top trade and could afford to weed out the customers she didn't want. I also believed what Abbot had said about better hookers improving the town. Except for Maggie's girls, getting rid of the ones who were here would be an improvement.

I had not forgotten my promise to see Sandy Lennon. I stopped at her place on my way back to Main Street and knocked at her front door, noting that she had lighted the lamp in her workroom.

She opened the door immediately and gave me a smiling welcome. "Come in, Marshal," she said.

I obeyed, and she shut the door behind me. I said: "I expect you about gave me up."

"No, I thought you would keep your word," she said. "When a complete stranger comes up to you, especially when you're weeding your garden and you have dirt on your face, and says he's going to marry you, I think you can depend on him."

I got red in the face. "That was pretty bold of me," I said, "but I meant it. I'll give you some time to get used to the idea."

"It's going to take a little time," she said. "Sit down. I have the coffee pot on the stove. I'll bring you a cup."

She left the room. I sat down in a rocking chair and leaned back and closed my eyes. I was tired, and my head hurt. It felt good just to sit here. I was surprised when I discovered I was relaxing.

I thought about this for a moment, remembering that I had been in a lot of places that tightened my nerves and made me want to leave. Here it was exactly the opposite. I felt at ease, the throbbing in my head began to slacken, and I realized I did not want to leave.

Sandy returned with two cups of coffee, handed one to me, and then sat down beside the cutting table, where she had been working on the blue velvet dress I had seen the day before. She sipped her coffee, looking at me over the rim of her cup.

"This was your first day as marshal, wasn't it?" she asked.

"Yes," I answered. "I made the rounds of the business places this afternoon. Tonight I met all of your customers. Outside of the Golden Palace, the women are a poor lot. I'm surprised you can make a living working for them."

"I'd starve if it wasn't for the Golden Palace," she said. "How are you feeling?"

"Fine," I said. "Just sitting here makes me feel better."

She set her cup down on the table. "I don't see how you could, surrounded by all of this female gimcrackery." She motioned to the dress. "I have to finish this by Saturday afternoon. The dress is for a girl named Rosebud. I don't suppose you picked her out from the others. You saw so many."

"I picked her out, all right," I said. "She called me a liar."

"I'm not surprised," Sandy said. "She gives Maggie a lot of trouble, but I understand she's popular with the men. This makes the other girls jealous."

"I can understand that," I said. "About this female gimcrackery you were talking about. That's not what makes me feel better. It's your company."

She picked up her coffee cup, her face flushing. "You are a clever man, Marshal. I don't think I can trust you."

"You can trust me," I said, "and I don't think I'm clever. I just wanted you to know how I felt. It's unusual. I was thinking about it when you were getting the coffee. It's not often that I am at peace with the world around me. I lived with violence in Clearwater, and I suppose I'll be living with it here."

"I'm afraid you will," she said. "There has been a great deal of it here. Miles City is still suffering from frontier growing pains."

"It will continue to feel them for a while," I said. "Sandy, what do you know about Joe Abbot?"

She looked at me sharply, as if wondering why I had asked,

and whether she could trust me. She said: "You know, don't you, that if I said anything against him, he could put me out of business?"

"I guess he could," I said, "seeing as he owns the Golden Palace."

"That's right," she said. "I don't know anything against him. I mean, more than you've heard. Maggie told you about how he treats the new girls?"

I nodded. "That's why I asked."

"The only other thing I could tell you is that I've had trouble convincing him that I don't need a man."

"That's about what I expected," I said. "If you ever need any help convincing him, let me know." I rose, aware that I had been here long enough for my first visit. "Thanks for the coffee. I'd better make my rounds before Bill Dillon comes to take my place. I'd like to call again, if I may."

"Of course you may," she said. "You are going to court me, aren't you?"

"Certainly," I said. "I can't marry you unless I court you, can I?"

We laughed. I picked up my hat and left, suddenly aware that for the moment I had completely forgotten my headache.

Chapter Eight

My first few weeks on the job were relatively quiet. I was thankful for that. It gave me a chance to get acquainted with the Miles City people, and that, in turn, gave me a fair idea of what they expected from their law officers. This is important, because no lawman can be effective unless he responds to the desires of the people he is hired to protect.

I had several talks with Abe Calder and Doc Lewis. When I asked about Joe Abbot, they turned mum quickly and suddenly. As far as I was concerned, I was perfectly happy to avoid Abbot. We should have had a complete understanding when I was hired. I thought, at the time, that we had such an understanding, but as I looked back on our conversation in Wolf's Saloon, I had a feeling that Abbot had meant for me to understand that he gave the orders.

That had not been said in plain words, but I sensed that it was the feeling Abbot wanted to convey. I wasn't going to stand still for it, and the sooner the problem came into the open, the better, but the opportunity for bringing it into the open didn't come around for a long time.

If Abbot and I met on the street, we spoke and that was all. He probably regretted already that I had been hired, and I didn't doubt that he would try to fire me on the first pretext he could find.

One of the occasions I had to get used to was pay day at the fort. The soldiers, or swaddies as they were called locally, flowed into Miles City like a tidal wave and practically took over the town. Women stayed off the streets. The businessmen were almost as inconspicuous as the women and avoided the saloons that were popular with the soldiers, particularly the Cottage Saloon on the corner of Fifth and Main.

Fights broke out as soon as the soldiers started drinking. I let them alone, thinking that fighting was their way of working off the boredom of garrison life, but if one of them started bullying a civilian, I interfered immediately.

My first problem came in the shape of Sergeant Rufe Hannegan. I'd heard about him, as you always hear about men who are a cut above the average. He was at least that, standing well over six feet and weighing about 220 pounds. He was broad-shouldered and had the reputation of being the toughest and meanest barroom brawler in all of Fort Keogh. The other soldiers were afraid of him, and with good reason.

I met him one afternoon about a month after I started wearing the star. He was in the middle of Main Street, waving a whiskey bottle around and crowing like a rooster. No one was challenging him, but he wasn't going to be satisfied until he found a fight.

A couple of hide hunters who had just got to town gave Hannegan his chance. They were a little drunk, I guess, drunk enough not to be careful. Or maybe they thought two of them could handle Hannegan. Anyhow, he baited them with a few choice insults, and they took him up. It was only a matter of seconds until he had knocked both of them cold.

I would have let him alone if he hadn't started to bang their heads together, making a sharp crack you could hear half a block away. I couldn't stand for that, so I walked into the street and told him to go back to the Cottage Saloon and behave himself. He probably had been working to get at me all the time. He didn't pretend to obey me. He let out a bellow that could have been heard clean to the fort, pawed the ground like an enraged bull, and charged me.

He expected me to give ground, I guess, or maybe to run. I simply side-stepped and slugged him on the ear as he went past. He went down, grunted, cursed, and kicked up a cloud of dust as he got to his feet.

He stood there for a moment, glaring at me, his mouth open, spit running down his chin. He came at me a second time. I didn't side-step or back up. I let him have it right on the jaw, and he went down in a pile. I grabbed him by the shoulders and dragged him to the nearest horse trough and rammed his head into the water.

Hannegan came to in a hurry. He gulped and choked and spit water and tried to curse me. I said: "I ought to drown you. Now, you get over to the saloon and do your drinking and let people alone."

He went, water dripping off his head and a coating of street dust over the front of his uniform. By this time half of the people of Miles City were on the sidewalk watching. I don't now whether Hannegan was aware of that or not. He didn't look back. He disappeared into the Cottage Saloon, and I thought that was the end of it.

The men on the sidewalk returned to their places of business. In one way it was a good thing, because I earned a lot of respect by handling Hannegan that way. The talk would get around, and probably save me some trouble later on.

I wasn't aware that Joe Abbot was standing behind me until he said: "You should have jailed him, Marshal."

I turned, and there he was, tall and skinny, with a kind of overbearing attitude, as if I were a lackey and he was lord of the manor. I hadn't had that impression the day they hired me, but I had it now, and I figured he was aiming to show me where I stood. Of course, I stiffened and got mule-headed, determined to show him I aimed to handle my job in my own way.

"I'll make my own judgment about things like that," I said coldly. "I thought we had that understanding."

"Our understanding did not exclude me giving you some advice," Abbot said, his tone just as cold as mine. "I know that big bastard. You're not done with him."

"Then I'll handle him when the time comes. I'll do it my own way," I said.

I didn't give him another chance to tell me what to do. I simply walked past him and went into Wolf's Saloon. Pete Green was sitting at his table with Lucky. He waved at me when I came in. He said: "That little lesson from Joe Abbot was overdue, Dave. He didn't talk tough when they hired you. He figured the time for tough talk was later."

"You didn't hear what he said just now," I told him. "His talk wasn't so tough."

"You'll hear him again," Green said, "and next time his talk will be tougher. Everybody in Miles City hears Joe Abbot."

Lucky was watching me, smiling a little. She asked: "Scared, Dave?"

"Yeah," I said. "Scared to death."

She laughed aloud. "Listen to him lie to me, Pete. Right to my face."

Green was tapping the green table top with the tips of his fingers. He said: "I've got a hunch you're just mean enough and tough enough to make it on your own. The way you handled Hannegan would indicate that, but Abbot's another problem. You don't handle him the way you do Hannegan."

"There's one thing I don't savvy," I said. "Abbot's got this burg buffaloed. Why?"

"I told you before not to buck him," Green said. "Nobody does."

"I do," I said, and walked to the bar and ordered a drink.

There was some kind of overpowering, Satanic quality about Joe Abbot that I simply did not understand. He wore several hats, and one of them was a crown. At least, he figured it was, and somehow he had convinced a lot of people in Miles City that he was big enough and smart enough to wear it.

I turned and started toward the door. A soldier stood there, staring at me as if he wasn't real sure he wanted to see me. He didn't move out of the way or say anything until I was about two steps away from him. Then he said: "You're Marshal Harmon, ain't you?"

"Yes."

"Sergeant Hannegan sent me over here to tell you that he's going to kill you, and he says you're too big a coward to come into the Cottage Saloon and get him."

"Oh, he's dead right," I said. "He scares the hell out of me."

I put out a hand and pushed the soldier to one side and walked out of the saloon. I knew I had to go after Hannegan, and I also knew that, if I went into the Cottage Saloon through the front door and let that crowd of soldiers at me, they'd tear me apart.

I'd been in the Cottage Saloon on days like this and had seen how the soldiers crowded the place from one wall to the other. The bartenders didn't try to serve their customers from the bar, but poured beer into two big washtubs and dipped it out of the tubs. The owner of the Cottage Saloon must have made a fortune every pay day.

I crossed Main Street, walking slowly, as if I were just making my usual round this time of day and not paying any attention to the Cottage Saloon. I knew they were watching, and I knew that they thought I had received the message and was afraid to come in.

When I reached the end of the block, I cut in behind Red Ward's Vaudeville House and ran along the alley until I reached the back door of the Cottage. I opened it and stepped into a storeroom that was nearly filled with beer barrels.

I threaded my way through the barrels to the door that opened into the saloon, shoved it back an inch or two so I had a crack to look through, and in a matter of seconds located Hannegan at the bar, his back to me. He was facing the front door, maybe expecting me to come in that way. A number of soldiers stood between me and Hannegan, but they weren't packed solid. I knew I could go through them, and I did, spilling them on both sides of me like tenpins.

I reached Hannegan before he realized what was happening. He heard enough commotion to make him turn just as I got to him. I rammed the muzzle of my Colt into his gut. I said: "This gun is cocked, Hannegan. It has a hair-trigger that fires with just a little pressure. If you or some of these men jostle me, you'll have a piece of raw lead to digest."

His face was red-veined from drinking too much, but, when I said that, it turned as pale as it was possible for it to be. He didn't say a word, and he didn't move. I said: "Hannegan, we're walking to the back door, and we're going through it. If you want to live, you'll keep your men off my back. Savvy?"

I stepped back one pace, and grabbed a shoulder and yanked him half around, and then rammed my gun against his spine. I said: "Move."

He did. The men in front parted, and we had a clear lane to the back door. I heard some movement behind us. I said: "Better stop 'em, Hannegan."

"Stand pat!" he yelled.

I didn't hear any more movement. We went through the storeroom into the alley and turned between the Cottage Saloon and Bach's restaurant into Fifth Street.

Chapter Nine

Jeff Munro walked into my office about a week after my run-in with Sergeant Hannegan. He shook hands with me and greeted me warmly. He said: "I hear you're doing a top-notch job."

"I'm not so sure." I motioned to a chair. "Sit down and tell me all about your trip."

He sat down across the room from me, took a cigar out of his pocket, bit off the end, and held a match flame to it. He puffed for a moment, looking at me through the smoke, then he said: "To be honest about it, I had a hell of a good hunting trip, and that was about all. I didn't find a ranch site I wanted, so I'll go back to the Judith Basin and quit looking. My backers will have to be satisfied with one outfit."

"If you had a good hunting trip, I guess the time wasn't wasted," I said.

"No, it wasn't wasted," he agreed. "I enjoy just about anything I do. I never consider time wasted, even if I don't accomplish what I set out to do. Well, how do you like Miles City by this time?"

"All right," I said. "What do you know about Joe Abbot?"

The question took him aback a little. He removed the cigar from his mouth and rolled it between his fingertips, his eyes boring into me. Then he said: "Why do you ask?"

"Because I figured you would know something about him," I said. "He's a mystery to me. He seems to figure he's the high muckety-muck in town, though I don't subscribe to any such notion. He owns a store which is respectable, a whorehouse which isn't, though it is the best we have, and he's got a horse ranch a mile or so below town, but he never does any ranching. Now, you add it up."

"Nothing to add up." He pulled on his cigar. "You know as well as I do that men on the frontier don't live the way they do in the East or on the coast. He's just got a variety of businesses. That's all. Respectable or not respectable has got nothing to do with it."

"Sure, sure," I said. "You're like everybody else in this town. They duck whenever I ask a straight question. Now, give me a straight answer. You can afford to. You don't live here."

He took the cigar out of his mouth and stared at it thoughtfully. "You know, Dave, I guess I don't know what you're talking about."

I was getting pretty sore by then. I said: "Jeff, you know damned well what I'm talking about. What kind of a man is Joe Abbot? How has he managed to buffalo the town the way he has?"

"Oh, that's what you want to know." Munro put the cigar back into his mouth again and pulled on it. "I figured that was what you wanted to know, so I guess I'll have to tell you, but I'll admit I hate to put it into words. Not that I'm afraid of him. It's just that he's got a lot of wires he can pull. Not only here in Miles City, but all over the territory. I guess that's the real reason nobody wants to tangle with him. Our friend Pete Green has told you, he says."

I nodded. "I'll ask you again. What kind of a man is he?"

Munro grinned. "You are a persistent bastard. All right, I'll tell you. He's a back-shooting son-of-a-bitch. He don't like to be crossed. Nobody knows where he came from or what he used to do or how he made his money, and he sure keeps a tight lip. I'll tell you one thing. Don't owe him any money. Or if you do, pay it back on time."

"What about this rumor that he's hand in glove with the

toughs, and he sells horses to anyone on the run who needs a fresh animal, and that he'll even hide a wanted man if he gets paid for it?"

"I believe it," Munro said, "though I don't know it for a fact. I had a talk with him and Calder and Doc Lewis about hiring you before I left. I figured it was time Miles City grew up a little, and it needed a good man wearing the star. Bill Dillon's all right. He just ain't the kind of man who'll stand up under pressure, and you're bound to get pressure in a town like this. We'll have it for a while, too."

He paused, as if reluctant to go on. I said: "You haven't made your point yet."

"No, I didn't," he admitted. "You see, I told them all that, and they agreed, though Abbot got a little skittish, saying they didn't want too tough a lawman because it would give the town a bad name of being too strict. It was easy enough to know what he was boogered about. He was afraid you'd be too much for him to handle. I'm nothing but a god-damned hypocrite, Dave. I knew that, if you took the star, sooner or later you'd bump heads with Abbot and you'd trim him down, but I told them you'd listen to reason."

"Looks to me like you're a pretty slick customer," I said. "You want him out of town, and you figure I can do it."

"That's right, Dave, absolutely right," Munro said blandly, "though it ain't so much I want him out of town. I just don't want him having so much to say about things. I ain't afraid to prophesy that this will never be a good town as long as Abbot rides as high as he is. Somebody's got to cut him down to size. I would do the job, if I lived here, but I get to Miles City about once a year, and that don't give me no right to interfere."

"Just how do you think I'll do it?" I demanded.

"I dunno, but you'll find a way. Two men like you and

Abbot can't stay in the same town and both run it. It's got to be one or the other of you. I'm banking on it being you." He rose and shook hands with me. "It's time I got back to the Judith Basin. I've been away too long now."

He left my office, striding up the street in that powerful, dignified way he had. I had a hunch he was using me, that he'd got me the job here expecting to use me for his own ends. I was surprised to discover that I didn't mind.

I was convinced that Jeff Munro was almost always on the right side and Joe Abbot was always on the wrong side. Still, I wasn't one to hunt for trouble. I decided I'd better have a talk with Mr. Joe Abbot. I put on my hat and walked down the street to the Mercantile before I could change my mind.

Abbot was in the front of the store unpacking cans of fruit and stocking the shelves when I came in. I never bought my groceries there. To tell the truth, I hadn't been in the store three times since I came to Miles City. Abbot stopped work and stared at me as if frozen. He was surprised, of course, and maybe a little scared, although I'm inclined to discount that.

"Howdy, Marshal," Abbot said.

"Howdy, Joe," I said. "I'd like to talk to you."

I glanced around the store while Abbot hesitated. Several customers were here. I could see three clerks waiting on them. There may have been more in the back room. I brought my gaze back to Abbot and saw that he was still standing half bent over, his hands full of cans. He straightened up slowly, set the cans on a shelf, and nodded toward the back of the store.

"We'll go to my office, which ain't much of an office," he said. "I just never got around to putting up a partition."

I followed him to the corner he had indicated. He didn't have much furniture for an office, but it apparently was all he needed: a roll-top desk, two straight-backed chairs, and a

70

good-size safe set against one wall. Abbot took the chair nearest the desk and motioned to the other one.

I sat down, suddenly wondering why I was there. I had come on impulse, and now that I had obeyed the impulse, I didn't know what to say. Abbot sat there, tall and ungainly, his hands on his thighs, his Adam's apple bobbing up and down every time he swallowed.

"I've heard a lot of stories about you," I said. "I don't know what to believe."

"Don't believe any of 'em," he said. "I'm the most-lied-about man in Miles City."

"What about the story that you're the biggest man in the country and you don't like to be crossed?"

This was good enough for openers. Abbot was confused. I had trouble identifying him as the subject of the worst stories I'd heard, such as beating the new girls in the Golden Palace. But I knew that appearances don't tell anything about a man, that sometimes a man was a coward personally but could still handle the men he'd hired.

"Just why did you come in here?" Abbot demanded after a long pause.

"Mostly to find out where you stand," I said. "If I'm going to be marshal, I aim to run my department. I've heard that you expect to give orders. After you jumped me the other day about Sergeant Hannegan, I decided I'd better get a few things straight."

"All right," Abbot said. "I'll tell you straight out that I think we hired the wrong man. I think you're too tough and too strict, and I think you'll be dead before Christmas if you stay on the job."

"You intend to get me fired?"

Abbot was looking at me, but he wasn't looking at me. I remembered how it had been in Wolf's Saloon the day they

71

hired me, how Abbot had appeared to be looking at me but was really looking past me to something on the wall behind me. He was doing exactly the same thing now. I'd had my doubts about him then, but they were worse now. I was convinced he couldn't be trusted.

"I don't think it will be necessary to fire you," he said. "You'll get killed, or you'll go after the wrong man and public opinion will make it necessary for you to quit. I remember you said the day we hired you that you wouldn't be hard to get rid of."

"I said it, all right, but I meant when the town turned against me, not when one man who has conflicting interest wants me out, and a man who doesn't want the law enforced, at that."

"I'll be the first to admit that I have conflicting interest," Abbot said, "but you'll find I'm not alone. There's a delicate balance here, and you're not trying to find it."

"No, and I'm not going to." I leaned forward, trying to catch his eyes, and failing. "You wanted Hannegan locked up. That makes me wonder why you told Bill Dillon to release the three men who beat up Jeff Munro and me."

Abbot shrugged. "Simple. I saw no sense in feeding them and going through the mockery of a trial. Men get beaten up every day in Miles City, and you don't arrest anyone. Why should we hold those men? They didn't kill you."

"You know damned well they would have," I said angrily. "They should have been tried for attempted murder, and I don't thank you for letting them go. But that's past and done with. It's the future I'm thinking about. I want it understood that I'm running my end of the show. I sure thought I made that plain the day I was hired."

"All right, you run it," he said, suddenly as angry as I was, "and you can take the full responsibility. Don't come bellyaching to me for help when you've overstepped your place."

"The last thing I'd do is to come running to you for help," I said. "I've got a hunch I'll be here a hell of a lot longer than you will."

I got up and walked out, knowing I hadn't accomplished much, if anything, although I may have cleared the air some. There wasn't much I could do now except wait for events to bring us to a showdown, and I was dead sure they would.

Chapter Ten

The best thing that happened to me that fall was my growing friendship with Sandra. I had no right to expect what happened. Actually it was beyond my wildest dreams. As I looked back upon my first meeting with her and what I said that day in her garden, it struck me that I had been just plain stupid.

I meant it, but it's a wonder I didn't get shut out of her life forever. However, I do believe it worked in my favor. Maybe my approach intrigued her. At any rate, I made a habit of dropping into her place at least once a day, my excuse being that as marshal I wanted to know if she was having any trouble and if there was anything I could do for her.

She always made me feel welcome. There were other men who called on her, but she always seemed cool to them and never invited them back. It was the opposite with me. Still, I was careful. I didn't want to rush her off her feet or to appear too eager.

Sometimes I was at her place only a minute or two. After such a brief visit she always seemed sorry to see me leave. At other times, when I could stay longer, she'd ask me to sit down, then she'd bring me a cup of coffee, and she'd work on a dress while I sipped my coffee.

On those occasions we would often sit for five minutes at a time without either of us saying a word. This was one of the many qualities she had that I liked. She didn't have to keep her tongue wagging all the time, as so many women did. It seemed strange, and I had never experienced this with any other woman, but I had a feeling that even in the silence we were communicating.

Several times I ran into one of the girls from the Golden Palace who was there for a fitting. They were not embarrassed if I sat down and watched, even if they were less than half clothed. Sandy wasn't embarrassed, either. I wondered about it, being dead certain that no other man would have been permitted to sit there the way I was. One time I asked Sandy about it.

"You're accepted," she said. "That's all. I like to have you here. So do the girls. They aren't afraid of you." She glanced at me questioningly, then said: "I take it from what the girls say that you never do any business with them."

"That's right," I said. "I don't."

She lowered her glance to her dress again and smiled, as if she was holding a pleasant secret to herself. She said: "This may surprise you, but the truth is the girls are actually afraid of men. Some men, anyway. I think Joe Abbot is the reason. As far as I know, none of the other men in town is like Abbot, but the girls never know for sure, or when a man will start being that way. Maggie tries to protect them, but there's only so much she can do."

Sandy worked in silence for a moment, then she said: "There's another thing you may not know. You made friends with all of them the first day you took the star when you said that, if they ever needed you, all they had to do was to send for you. Too many lawmen take advantage of their job and expect to get the girls' services free. Or else they look at the girls as if they are so many animals and feel they have no right to expect protection. What I'm saying is that they appreciate what you said that day."

"I haven't been any help to them yet," I said.

"But they believed you, and they were sure that, when the day comes that they have to call on you, you won't let them down." She worked for a time in silence, frowning, then she said slowly: "Dave, there's something I think I should tell you. I haven't, because I just wasn't sure that I should, but I've decided I will."

"I'm no blabbermouth, if that's what you're worried about," I said.

"No, no." She threw her head back and laughed, then turned grave. "That wasn't what I was thinking at all. It's just that I have always despised people who tell things that have been told to them in confidence, and I don't like despising myself."

"Then don't tell me," I said.

She shook her head. "I'm going to, because I think it's important for you to know. Four or five years ago Lucky was working in a house in Denver. She was Joe Abbot's woman."

"What?" I stared at her, not believing it, and thinking it was the wildest thing I'd ever heard. "That couldn't be."

"It's true, although I should qualify what I said. Abbot didn't want to take care of her or have her keep house for him. He just wanted her when he came to the house, and he always asked for her. She never said he beat her. Maybe he hadn't started that yet. Anyhow, Lucky got along with him all right, but she said she never liked him. Then Pete showed up, and she ran off with him.

"They went to Cheyenne, and then to Deadwood, and wound up here, not knowing that Abbot was in Miles City. They were both surprised, shocked, I guess, to find him already in business here, but neither would leave because of Abbot. He ignored them at first, then he began suggesting to Lucky that she leave Pete and come to the Golden Palace. At first she didn't tell Pete. Then she began to worry after hearing some of the stories the girls told about Abbot, so she told Pete. He went right to Abbot and said he'd kill him the next time he opened his mouth to Lucky about going to work in the Golden Palace."

I sat there, listening to every word, finding the whole story hard to believe. I said: "Pete keeps telling me that nobody bucks Abbot. I don't savvy that. Looks to me like he's bucking him."

"It's a stand-off," Sandy said. "He knows that Abbot is powerful. They hate each other, and you'll never see Abbot playing poker at Pete's table. Pete knows that Abbot has connections with the toughs, and he doesn't want to make enemies of them. Right now they ignore each other, but I think that, if both of them stay in Miles City, Pete's going to kill Abbot."

"That's why you thought you ought to tell me," I said.

She nodded. "That's right. I know you won't tell Lucky, so she won't know I betrayed her confidence. Maybe you can't stop it. Maybe you won't even try, but it seemed to me it was the kind of situation that could lead to bigger trouble."

"It could," I said. "I'm still not sure about Abbot. Sooner or later I'm going to have it out with him. Did Lucky say what Abbot was doing in Denver? I've wondered how he got his start."

"She didn't know for sure," Sandy said, "but he was involved with some kind of mining deal. As far as she could tell, he was buying high-grade ore that the miners had stolen, and he was reselling it in Denver. A go-between, I guess you'd call him."

"He could have made a fortune that way," I said.

After that I always looked at Pete Green with a little more understanding. Abbot seldom went into Wolf's Saloon, and, if he did, I noticed that he and Pete made a point of ignoring each other. Lucky would sometimes shoot a quick glance at Abbot, then bring her gaze back to Green. I wondered what she was thinking, how she compared the two men.

She had known both of them intimately. She was bound to think of her situation, tied to a man she knew she could not depend on, and yet she must have felt she was better off than having anything to do with a man like Joe Abbot.

The longer I was in Miles City and the more I saw of Abbot, the more I disliked him. Stories kept popping up about him. He never did anything I could arrest him for, or that I could prove, but, as far as I could tell, none of the other businessmen trusted him.

I was reminded of what Jeff Munro had said, that if I ever owed Abbot any money, I'd better pay it back on time. This was the kind of story that people told about him most often, how he never gave an inch if anyone owed him five cents. If he couldn't collect, there always seemed to be some plug uglies around who gave the man who owed Abbot a beating. After that, the man always found some way to repay Abbot.

Sometimes the hardcases got out of town before I caught them, and sometimes I didn't know who to go after, because the man who got the beating was too terrified to name his assailants. If I did arrest them and throw them into jail, they'd be fined, they'd pay because they always had money, and they'd walk out of the jail and thumb their noses at me or Bill Dillon.

I was convinced that the men who jumped Jeff Munro and me were hardcases that Abbot had sent for. That was why he had insisted that Bill Dillon release them. He never made any such request of me because he knew it wouldn't do any good.

One day, not long after my talk with Abbot, Abe Calder saw me walk by his store and called to me. I turned back, and he stepped out on the boardwalk. He said: "I don't see you very often, Marshal. I mean, to talk to, but I've watched you, and I've heard people talk about you. I want you to know that we're pleased with the way you're handling your job, and we hope you're satisfied enough to stay."

"I am," I said. "I haven't bought any property here yet, but I will. It's like you and the others said that day you hired me. Miles City is going to be a good town."

"You bet it is," he said. "I'll give you a tip. There are some lots along the railroad right-of-way that are for sale. We'll have the Northern Pacific in here soon, as you know. You can buy those lots for a fair price now, but they'll be going up. . Why don't you see Pearly Means about buying them?"

I knew Pearly Means, a real-estate dealer. I nodded and said: "I will."

"Good," Calder said. "Once you own property here, you'll have your roots down. Take Jeff Munro. He'll always be a cattleman until he gets too old to work at it, and his ranch is a long ways from here, but he believes in Miles City, and he owns a good deal of property here. I think he really considers it his town."

"I guess not everybody is satisfied with my work," I said.

"Nobody can satisfy everybody," Calder said grimly. "That's why I stopped you. Joe Abbot is doing some talking, but he won't get anywhere. Don't pay any attention to him. As a matter of fact, he doesn't carry as much weight as he thinks he does."

That afternoon I bought the lots from Pearly Means. I thought about what Calder had said. It occurred to me that people, Pete Green in particular, made more of Abbot's power than they should. I never ran into anybody who liked him, but then I never talked much with the hardcases who were in and out of town. I'm sure they would have given me a different slant on Abbot.

Anyhow, I was glad that Calder had said what he had, and I felt that, as far as the law-abiding element went, I had no worry about my job. Not that I cared about it one way or the other, but I wanted to stay in Miles City. The more I saw of Sandy, the more I thought of her, and that, I think, was the only good reason I wanted to stay.

One quiet afternoon, about a week after my talk with Calder, I was having a drink in Wolf's Saloon when Lucky came to the bar and stood beside me. She said: "I don't see you as much as I'd like, Marshal. I thought we were going to be such good friends."

"We are," I said. "I'm not forgetting how you treated me when I first got here. Or Pete, either."

"I hope you won't forget about Pete," she said. "He's got one life coming."

"Did he send you over to tell me that?" I asked.

"Hell, no," she said quickly. "I came over here to tell you that you know more about women than I gave you credit for. I thought from the crazy way you started with Sandy, you had cut your own throat, but you didn't."

"Well?"

"Well, damn it," she said in an irritated tone, "you're ace high with her."

"I didn't know that," I said.

She threw up her hands. "You're more stupid than I thought. You're one step away from heaven, and you don't even know it."

I wasn't real sure what she meant, and I didn't pursue it. I was involved with her and Pete Green all I wanted to be. The proper person to take it up with was Sandy herself, and that was exactly what I did.

Chapter Eleven

The Northern Pacific built into Miles City in November. The town celebrated, but it seemed to me that it did not put on the big shindig that other towns like Cheyenne had. Maybe it was because the railroad had been stalled so long in Bismarck.

Still, it was a big occasion when the rails reached town and we all knew it meant a great deal for the mail service into Miles City, as well as the passenger and freight service. It meant, too, that we were not dependent on high water for the boats to reach us with freight, or the stagecoaches and bull trains the rest of the year.

Late in the month I received an invitation that read like this:

NPRR

Your presence is requested at Headquarters of Engineering Department, Yellowstone Division, NPRR, at Miles City, November 24, 1881, at 2 p.m. to join with the Engineers of the Division at a Thanksgiving Dinner.

$\qquad\qquad$ **Yours cordially,**

$\qquad\qquad$ **J. P. Clough**

$\qquad\qquad$ **ENG. YELLOWSTONE DIV.**

R.S.V.P.

I was never one for parties, but I couldn't miss this. I accepted immediately.

On Thanksgiving morning I got a bath, shave, and haircut at Pruitt's barbershop on Main Street. Pruitt stayed open just to accommodate us. I had to wait for my bath water to heat, because several were ahead of me. As soon as I got done, I went home, put on my one white shirt and my one brown broadcloth suit, and went to Sandy's place.

As usual, she was working on a dress. She gasped when she saw me, then got up and came to me and took my hands. She said: "Your lordship, may I ask what the occasion is?"

I told her, and then, because I could not put it off any longer, I said: "Sandy, will you marry me?"

She gasped again, and for a long time stood there looking up into my face, then suddenly the tears began running down her cheeks.

"Wait a minute," I said. "This isn't an occasion that calls for tears. At least, I didn't aim for it to be."

"Oh, it isn't, Dave," she whispered. "I guess it's just that I'm so happy."

I kissed her, long and hard, and, after I'd let her go, she put her face against my chest and kept on crying. A moment later she drew back and said: "I'm messing up your suit." She went back to her cutting table and sat down. She wiped her eyes and motioned for me to come and take a chair opposite her.

I sat down, asking: "When you said you were so happy, you were saying yes, weren't you?"

She wiped her eyes again and swallowed. "No, it doesn't mean that. I've got something to tell you. I should have told you a long time ago." She swallowed again. "I knew you were going to ask me to marry you. I guess I've known it ever since that day when you came into my back yard and you said you were going to marry me. It was the craziest thing that ever happened to me, but I honestly thought you meant it. The funny part of it is that I liked what I saw of you, even though I thought you were a madman.

"If you had pressed me right away, I'd have locked the

82

door when I saw you coming, but you didn't. You never even kissed me till just now. You've always been a gentleman, Dave. I think I fell in love with you within a week. All the time I've wanted you to ask me to marry you, and yet I never knew what I'd say when you did. Now I know. I've got to tell you."

She scared me. I sat there looking at her, my imagination running away with me. I could think of a dozen reasons that she could give me for not marrying her, none of them good, but certainly her *no* did not come from her not wanting to marry me. So I waited for her to go on talking. It took her a little time. She stared at her hands on her lap, the corners of her mouth twitching, then she looked at me.

"I can't marry you, Dave, because I'm already married," she blurted. "I don't want to go to jail for bigamy."

That was one reason I had not thought of. It jolted me. I said: "I thought. . . ." I stopped. I thought she was single. She didn't wear a ring. Then I realized she had never told me she wasn't married, and I also remembered Lucky's saying that Sandy had not said anything about her life before she had come here.

"I know what you thought," Sandy said, "and I should have told you, but I didn't want to. I . . . I didn't want to stop you from coming to see me. I was married when I was just a girl, a child really. I had been living with my mother and step-father in a mining camp about forty miles out of Boise. My home was hell, and, when I had a chance to marry, I jumped at it just to get away from home, but what I really did was to jump from the frying pan into the fire.

"I guess my husband was like Joe Abbot. At first he was good to me, but he wasn't making anything out of his claim, and he was using up all the money he'd saved. He got mean and began to beat me. I stood it for a while. I thought he'd get over it, but he got worse, so one morning right after he went to work I stole part of his money. I thought I had it coming after the way he treated me, but I never forgave myself for it. Later, I sent it back to him, but I don't know whether or not he got it.

"Anyhow, I had enough to get me to Denver, where I worked for a while, then I went to Omaha, and from there to Bismarck. I came here on a boat two years ago, and I stayed, because I wanted to live somewhere. I was tired of running around."

She stopped. I just sat there, thinking that after all of my running around and never finding a woman I wanted, it was a hell of a note to find Sandy and then have her tell me she was already married.

She didn't say anything more. That was all, I guess, all that she wanted to say, at least. I suppose she thought I'd rant and rave around, but I didn't. I asked: "Why didn't you get a divorce?"

"At first I never had the slightest idea I'd want to get married," she said. "I'd never liked men. Maybe I've been afraid of them. I don't know. Anyhow, it never occurred to me that there was any reason for me to get a divorce until you showed up last summer. I have talked to a lawyer, Eli Whitcomb. He said it would be hard and slow. I'd have trouble showing cause, because it happened a long time ago, and also because my husband wasn't known here. Besides, it would cost more than I can afford."

I sat there, not moving, just thinking about it. I guess I was a little stunned. Finally I said: "I'm not going to give you up, Sandy. I never thought I'd say that. Any woman I ever met I could get along without until I met you."

"I don't want you to give me up," she said. "Please keep coming to see me."

"Plenty of couples living together in Miles City are not

married," I said. "You know that as well as I do. It doesn't seem to bother anybody."

"I've thought about that," she said. "Believe me, I've thought about it a lot, because I knew this was coming, but I decided I didn't want to move in with you or have you move in with me so everybody in town knows about it. It wouldn't hurt my reputation, but it wouldn't do yours any good, because of your job."

I hadn't thought about it, but she was right. Ordinary people could sin all they wanted to and nobody thought much about it, but the marshal was not an ordinary person. It was partly a matter of law. Mostly, though, a town marshal had to be rough and tough dealing with lawbreakers, but his personal life was everybody's business. It was a little bit like it was with a teacher or a preacher. At least, that was the way it seemed to me.

Of course, I could find something else to do, but probably nothing that paid as well. I was saving money, and I was looking forward to the time when I could buy a ranch or at least some kind of business.

I sat there with all of this running through my mind, then Sandy said: "Dave."

She said it very softly. She was still staring at the dress on her lap. I said: "Yes?"

"I want to feel married to you," she said. "Maybe if people didn't know . . ."—she stopped, her face flushing, then she went on—"when you finish your shift at midnight, come along the alley to the back door. I'll leave it unlocked."

I wasn't shocked or even surprised, because I'd had the same idea, but I'd been afraid to say it. I said: "I don't like for you to leave your door unlocked. Sometimes drunks go along the alley just checking doors to see if they're locked or not."

"I'll keep it locked until almost midnight," she said.

"Besides, I have a pistol that I can keep right beside my bed."

It was time for me to go. I rose and put a hand under her chin and tipped her head back. I said: "I love you, Sandy." I kissed her and left the room. I may have been walking on air. Or maybe I was flying. I'm not sure. I thought the men at the dinner table would notice, but nobody mentioned it.

The dinner? Well, I doubt that there was a bigger or better dinner served anywhere in the whole world that Thanksgiving Day. It was unbelievable. I never expect to see such a variety of food again. Three kinds of soup; oysters—fried, scalloped, or raw; trout and salmon; nine kinds of meat, including elk and mountain sheep; six kinds of vegetables; five kinds of pie; six side dishes—mostly fruit; lemon and vanilla ice cream; and five kinds of cake.

We ate until we were uncomfortable. All of the important townsmen were there, along with a number of railroad men. Joe Abbot, of course, was one of the loudest talkers about the rosy future of Miles City, although the others, including the NP men, got in their two-bits' worth, all dwelling on the great future of our town. It got a little monotonous and boring along toward the end. Some of us, including me, fell asleep a few times during the oratory.

As soon as it was over, I hurried home, changed my clothes, and made the final round of the business blocks. When I reached the office, Bill Dillon was there.

"All quiet," I said.

"Everybody's too full of Thanksgiving dinner to be up to any meanness," Bill said.

"Looks like it," I agreed.

I left the office as if I were going home, then turned on Eighth to Bridge Street and followed it to the Golden Palace on the corner of Sixth and Bridge. I took the alley to the rear of Sandy's house, opened the back door, stepped inside, and closed the door.

I was in her bedroom. She was sitting up in bed, very much awake. A lighted candle was on a nightstand beside the head of her bed.

She said: "Lock the door."

I obeyed, then sat down on the edge of the bed, took off my clothes, and slid in beside her. She came to me at once, freely and without reservation, letting me know that she wanted me as much as I wanted her.

Chapter Twelve

As far as my job was concerned, the fall was relatively quiet. We had a deluge of cowboys when the big herds went through. There were always a few cowhands around anyhow, because ranches were being established on the Powder, the Tongue, and the Rosebud as well as the Yellowstone. Some were being started north of town, too, in an empty area that one of my friends called "the big open"—which was as good a name for it as anything.

By and large I got along with the cowboys. They kicked up some dust when they were in town, but most of it was good-natured rowdyism. A few were ornery, but most of them were decent and clean, and they certainly had great respect for what they called *good* women.

I think they respected the hookers, too, although in a different way. They gave all their business to the Golden Palace and stayed away from the other houses, which was what Maggie Adams had said they would do.

Once Maggie remarked: "I hope they get some more decent houses in this town. We've had a lot more cowboy business this year than last, and we'll have even more next year. I tell you, Dave, my girls had so much business this year they're worn to a frazzle."

"You may have to go to work yourself," I said.

She laughed and shook her head. "Not me. My working days are over."

"Why don't you start a place of your own, instead of working for Joe Abbot?" I asked.

"I'd like to, Dave," she said. "I sure would. I've thought

about it a lot. I've got some money, but not enough to buy a house or build one."

"Go see one of the bankers," I said. "You can show more profit than most of the businessmen who borrow from the bank. Now that we've got the railroad, Miles City will be the biggest cattle-shipping point in Montana."

That was part of the rosy railroad and Commercial Club talk, but I believed it. The shipping, of course, would bring more cowboys to Miles City.

Maggie nodded in agreement. "It makes sense. I believe I could pay off any reasonable loan in two, three years. I've got some ideas that skinflint Joe won't agree to because they'd cost him money."

"Go talk to John Bains, or any of the rest of them," I said. "Won't hurt to see what they say."

"You do it," she said. "I'm afraid to."

I was surprised at that, because I didn't think Maggie Adams was afraid of Old Scratch himself, but I guess I was wrong. That afternoon I dropped into Bains's bank and put it up to him. He chewed on his cigar and looked over his steel-rimmed spectacles at me until I finished.

"Are you putting any money in Maggie's establishment?" he asked.

"No," I said. "I used up my capital buying those lots on the railroad's right-of-way, but maybe I made a mistake. I'd get a quarter return on my investment with Maggie."

"Oh, you'll make some money out of those lots." He shook his head. "I'm sorry, Marshal, but I don't want to back Maggie. I can save you some trouble, too, by telling you that you will get the same answer from the other bankers."

I wanted to ask him how he knew so much about it, and then the answer hit me. I said: "You're afraid of Joe Abbot, aren't you?"

He squirmed around and scratched the back of his neck. Finally he said: "I wouldn't use the word 'afraid'. I know he wouldn't like it, and I see no point in antagonizing him."

"But if I invested my savings in her place, you might look at it differently," I said. "You figure that, if I invested personally, I'd keep Abbot in line, don't you?"

He ignored the question. "I can't give you a firm commitment, but, yes, in that case I would reconsider."

"I could borrow, using my lots as collateral, couldn't I?"

"You certainly could."

"I'll see Maggie," I said.

I did, but she wouldn't go ahead with it. "It just goes to show you that Joe Abbot can pull a lot of wires. I don't want to put you in a squeeze, Dave. If the bankers don't want to buck Joe, by God, I don't, either."

"Have you had any new girls lately?" I asked.

"What's that got to do with it?"

"I'm just asking."

"Well, yes, I took in a couple, but they weren't real young, and Joe decided he didn't need to test 'em out, if that's what you're getting at."

"Yeah, that's what I was getting at," I said.

So there it was again. I let it drop, but it graveled the hell out of me. I wasn't real sure, but I had a notion that men like John Bains figured Abbot would protect them if they played his game. On the other hand, if they bucked him, they'd get their banks held up.

I was just guessing, but Abbot wasn't a man to scare anybody personally. It must be his connection with the hardcases that boogered the businessmen. When I thought about it, I had to admit that, in the months I had been in Miles City, there had been no major crimes. I wondered if Joe Abbot could claim any credit.

Later in the year the hide hunters swarmed into town. I'd had some contact with them in Clearwater, but not as many as showed up in Miles City. I despised them. Some were decent, law-abiding citizens who kept themselves reasonably clean, but as a class they were a dirty, stinking lot.

It was a standing joke, and not much of a joke at that, that when two or three hide hunters bellied up to a bar in a saloon that catered to them, the last one to find a louse in his clothes paid for the drinks. A good many of the saloons such as Wolf's made it plain that they didn't want the hide hunters' business.

"We don't make any bones about it," Pete Green told me. "The stink is enough excuse for us to keep them out of here."

It made me mad, too, the way they were slaughtering buffalo for a measly $3.50 a hide or less, and letting almost all of the meat rot. The tongue might be saved, and that was about all, although a few Miles City butchers did bring some meat in and sell it for two or three cents a pound, but there was no way to preserve big amounts of meat for any long period of time, so there wasn't anything that could be done about saving it.

I remembered Jeff Munro telling me that he had ridden into Miles City in the spring of 1880 and had found the bodies of dead buffalo scattered all over the bottom land. They had been skinned and the hides stacked high on the ground. He guessed that 10,000 or more had been killed in the area in that one winter.

The southern herd had been nearly wiped out by the end of the 1875 hunting season, and now the hide hunters were here. I had no doubt that the northern herd would go the same way. I'd heard the argument, of course, that there wasn't enough grass for both the buffalo and the big herds of cattle that were moving in from Texas and Oregon.

I'd also heard a second argument, and I think it was the one that led to the wiping out of the buffalo. The government wanted the Indians corralled on the reservations, and they couldn't be kept there as long as the buffalo were on the plains. The buffalo was their living. Kill the buffalo, and the Indians were forced to come in for food or starve, so the government encouraged the hunters.

Well, the arguments were valid enough, I suppose, and we had reached the place where we wanted cattle on Montana grass, and we were tired of fighting Indians. The battle of the Little Big Horn and Miles's winter campaign and the Nez Percé business were fresh in the minds of the Miles City people. Even the Sioux and the Cheyennes who camped up the Tongue not far from Miles City made the townspeople nervous. Still, speaking personally, I hated to see the buffalo go.

For the time being, buffalo hunting brought business to our town. It was estimated that the hide and robe business put a quarter of a million dollars into circulation in the Miles City area. I could believe it.

For instance, hunting parties were not all of the same size, but each would have at least one hunter, two skinners, and a cook. When the hunting was top-notch, more skinners would be hired. A man would be paid fifty dollars a month, which he probably spent in town. An outfit would cost around $1,500 or more, and usually it would be bought in Miles City. All of this was short-range prosperity, and I'm sure everyone knew it, but businessmen were happy about it as long as it lasted.

I don't think anyone knew how many buffalo were killed around Miles City. *The Yellowstone Journal* claimed that in one year 180,000 hides were shipped from Custer County, which was the entire southeastern corner of the territory. The figure was a guess, of course, but it probably was as close as any.

I talked to a number of men who worked for the steamboat companies. They might have been trying to out-lie each other, but they all told the story of thousands of hides banked at every steamboat landing on the Yellowstone from Fort Buford to the Big Horn, and as far up as Fort Benton on the Missouri.

One of the things I learned that winter about buffalo was the fact that they were not all the same color, and that this had a great influence on the value of the hides. I had assumed they were all of the usual dark brown when the hide was prime, and I knew that later in the spring the color faded to a seal-brown, but besides this normal color there were a few very rare white ones, some buckskin, and a number of "blue", or mouse-colored, robes. A hunter told me that about one percent of the hides he brought in were blue. He got $16.00 for each of them.

Joe Abbot was one of the biggest local dealers. During the season he was a busy man, too busy to make any trouble or to keep talking me down around town as he had been doing. The result was that I saw very little of him.

Later, when the hunting season was over and the hides had been shipped, he apparently found time hanging on his hands. Maybe that was what brought on the trouble, a sort of Abbot-style celebration similar to the hell raising a cowboy does when he reaches town after a long drive.

Anyhow, one evening in early summer while I was eating supper with Sandy, the Golden Palace girl called Sunbeam ran in looking for me. She was out of breath and scared, and it took a while to understand what she wanted. It seemed that Maggie Adams had just taken on a new, young girl, and Joe

Abbot had sent word he would be over later in the evening to test her.

"I'll be here with Sandy," I said. "Have Maggie send for me if Abbot gives her any trouble."

I made my rounds before dark, then settled down for the evening with Sandy, figuring this was the night I'd known was coming ever since Maggie had told me about Joe Abbot.

Chapter Thirteen

Time passed very slowly. Sandy had a cuckoo clock on the wall that kept calling the hour and half hour, but between the cuckoos I turned my gaze to the clock every three minutes, wondering if it was still measuring time.

Sandy worked on a dress until her eyes gave out, then she just sat, sometimes looking at me and sometimes staring across the room at a blank wall. She kept the coffee hot and brought me a cup when I wanted it.

Once she said suddenly: "Dave, what will we find to talk about for a whole lifetime?"

I laughed, the first time I'd laughed in hours. What she'd said wasn't funny, but I had been under so much strain that I needed release, and I guess the laughter gave it to me. "I don't know," I said. "You think we shouldn't spend our lives together because we'd run out of things to talk about?"

She grimaced. "No, I don't think that, and I do want us to spend our lives together. Right now, I wish we could go to bed."

"So do I," I said, "but for once I'll have to discourage you."

"I know." She was silent a moment, then she asked: "What are you going to do, kill him?"

"It would be a pleasure," I said, "but I don't expect to indulge myself that much."

"I can't keep from worrying," she said. "You might have to kill him, and, if you do, you may have all of his tough friends trying to get revenge."

"Then I'll be in trouble," I said, "but I don't expect that to happen. I've wondered about his tough friends. Maybe it's all bluff. Abbot may have started the gossip just to scare everyone in town."

"You know better," she said. "There have been plenty of them in town at different times, and we know they were living at his ranch."

"There have been some around, all right," I said, "but they drift in and out. Right now, I don't know that any of them are at his ranch."

She got up and, walking to the door, stood looking into the street. "I worry about you, Dave," she said somberly. "Being a marshal is a dangerous job. You don't know from one day to the next what you have to face. What I'm trying to say is that we've known each other less than a year, but it's the only happy time I've ever had in my life. The thought that some killer might shoot you in the back on a dark night is more than I can stand."

I had never worried about anything like that happening and I hadn't suspected that Sandy did. I got up and went to her, but, before I could say a word, I heard a woman's running step on the boardwalk. I stepped outside. Sunbeam saw me and screamed: "He's doing it, Marshal. Hurry."

I ran past her to the Golden Palace. The front door was open. Maggie was in the hall, a shotgun in her hands. When she saw me, she yelled: "First door to your right at the head of the stairs. I was fixing to go up there and kill the bastard just like I told him I would."

I took the stairs three at a time. I heard the girl screaming while I was still on the stairs. Some of the doors down the hall were open; the girls were looking out, pale-faced and scared, and in that split second the thought flashed through my mind that some of them had probably gone through this with Joe Abbot.

I tried the door. It was locked. I stepped back and gave the door a good, hard kick. The flimsy lock gave way, and the door crashed open. Then I moved into the room.

I knew what I'd see, and yet, when I actually saw what was happening, I stopped, finding it unbelievable. A naked girl was on the bed writhing in agony, her back covered with long red welts. Some of them were bleeding. She was so small that I had a terrible feeling she was only a child.

Joe Abbot stood beside the bed, naked except for his boots. He held a leather strap in his right hand, and, even as I stood there frozen, he raised it and brought it down across the girl's back, making an audible snap as it lashed her flesh.

I had one glimpse of his face. I can't describe his expression. I had never seen anything like it, but I had the impression that he was in a state of ecstatic bliss. One thing was certain. He didn't know I was there.

As he raised the strap for another blow, I came out of it in time to grab his arm with one hand and twist the strap out of his grip with the other.

I yelled at the girl: "Get out of here!"

She rolled over, leaving blood on the blanket, fell off the bed to the floor, then scrambled to her hands and knees, and finally lunged upright and ran out of the room. I hit Abbot on the side of the head and knocked him across the bed. He fell belly down, and I let him have it across his back just as he had been beating the girl.

It was the first time in my life that I went completely crazy with fury. Abbot bellowed in surprise and pain and started to get up. I hit him on the back of his neck, and he fell across the bed. He didn't try to get up again. He lay on his belly, yelling bloody murder every time I hit him.

I don't know how many times I struck him with the strap. Afterward I didn't remember much of what happened, but I used the strap on him until I was tired. I wouldn't have quit then if Maggie hadn't come in and got hold of my arm, screaming at me: "That's enough, Dave. Don't beat him to death."

I stepped back and wiped the sweat off my face. Suddenly I was thinking and seeing again, the red haze of rage dying in me, and I saw that his back was worse off than the girl's had been. I threw the strap across the room.

"Abbot, can you hear me?" I asked.

He had his face pressed against the pillow, and he was gripping both ends of it. His body was shaking with sobs, but he wasn't making a sound. I said: "Abbot, if you can't hear me, I'm going to yank you right off that bed and take you down Main Street in the condition you're in now."

He moved his head enough to say: "I hear you."

"All right," I said. "Now, you listen damned good. If you ever do this again, I'll kill you. Do you savvy that?"

"I savvy," he said in a muffled voice.

Maggie still held my arm. Now she pulled me out of the room and closed the door. I leaned against the wall, so tired for a moment that I thought I couldn't move. I was weak and trembling, and for some crazy reason I felt like I wanted to cry.

"The bastard," Maggie said. "The god-damned bastard! I'm glad you got here when you did, Dave. I would have killed him as sure as snowballs melt in hell."

"How's the girl?" I asked.

"She'll be all right," Maggie said. "I've got Sunbeam and some of the others looking after her. Come on downstairs. You need a drink."

"I do, for a fact," I said.

I followed her down the stairs to her parlor. She poured me a stiff drink. I felt better then. I wiped my face again. It was wet with sweat. I said: "Maggie, he was crazy. He was clean out of his mind."

"I know," she said dully. "What's going to happen now?"

"I don't know," I said. "Why?"

"There'll be hell to pay in more ways than one," she said. "He's a proud man. He won't forget this."

"He won't put a gun on and face me," I said. "He hasn't got the guts."

"Something will happen," she said. "It's got to. He might close this place. He may sell the store. He may shoot you in the back. It wouldn't be hard, the way you prowl this town after dark."

"Let him try," I said. "All I know is that it won't take much to make me kill him, and he knows it."

I left then and returned to Sandy's place. I told her what had happened, and I discovered I was still shaking. She said: "Stay here, Dave. I'll go find Bill Dillon and tell him to take the last hour of your shift."

"No," I said. "I'll take it. It'll be good for me to walk."

"Dave." She put her hands on my shoulders and looked up at me. "I'll unlock the back door at midnight."

"No," I said. "Not tonight."

I spent the next hour walking the streets and alleys, but it didn't help. I kept seeing the bloody back of the girl and the expression on Abbot's face as he brought the strap down for another blow.

I didn't tell Bill Dillon what had happened when he came at midnight. I said—"It's all yours, Bill."—and went home and to bed.

Chapter Fourteen

As far as I knew, Joe Abbot did not leave the Golden Palace for a week. I had not expected him to perform that way. I stopped every evening and talked to Maggie. I wanted to know what he was doing, but mostly I wanted to keep a close tab on Maggie and the girl, because I had a hunch Abbot would take his fury out on them.

As the week passed, I found Abbot's actions more and more surprising, almost unbelievable, but I was sure Maggie was telling the truth. She swore that Abbot didn't even leave his room. She brought his meals to him and took care of his back. He was so sore he could hardly move, she said, but he refused to call Doc Lewis.

"It's his pride, Dave," Maggie said. "He'll stand at the window, or he'll lie in bed and not say anything and not do anything, but he's got the most whipped look on his face I ever saw on a human being. I almost feel sorry for him."

"Don't," I said. "Save your sympathy for the girls he beat."

"I know, Dave, I know," Maggie said. "The damned idiot brought it on himself. If you hadn't come and beat hell out of him, I'd have killed him, so he's lucky. I told him that, but he doesn't hear a thing I say."

"Keep your eye on him," I said. "He may go crazy again before he leaves there."

I had expected him to cuss me all day and swear he was going to get me as soon as he got on his feet, but Maggie insisted he never mentioned me. Later in the week she said he began talking about Pete Green and how much he hated him.

"I don't know why he should hate Green," Maggie said. "He doesn't go into Wolf's Saloon very often, from what I hear, and he don't play poker at Green's table. What's the matter with him, Dave?"

"They haven't seen much of each other since I've been here," I said, figuring there was no point in telling Maggie what Sandy had told me, "so it must be some old quarrel between them."

"He talks about that Lucky woman," Maggie said. "He says she's the most beautiful woman he ever saw and that she'd be a good madam. He looks at me, and his lips curl down like he had a bad taste in his mouth, and then he'll say she'd make a better madam than an old worn-out dog like me. I get so mad at the bastard that I feel like pulling his tongue out by the roots."

That gave me a little different slant on the whole picture. When I had a chance to see Lucky alone, I asked: "Has Joe Abbot ever propositioned you about taking the madam's job at the Golden Palace?"

She looked as guilty as sin. She swallowed and glanced around as if afraid Green might be close enough to hear her, then she said: "Don't you mention that to Pete. He'd kill Joe. He's got enough trouble without having to settle for killing a son-of-a-bitch like Joe Abbot."

"You're not answering my question."

She nodded. "He's spoken to me about it, and he's sent word in other ways that I can have the job anytime I want it."

"Did you encourage him?"

"Hell, no," she said sharply. "I don't want anything to do with Joe Abbot. I've told him that. He just can't take no for an answer."

"You'd better watch him if he comes in here," I said. "Maybe you'd better tell Pete. Abbot's gone clean off his rocker, if I'm any judge."

"I've been wondering." She frowned. "He must be up to something. I've heard some of the men say he hasn't been in his store for several days."

I didn't tell her what had happened. I thought it was just as well if she didn't know, but I still worried about what Abbot would do. For him to turn his bitterness from me to Pete Green didn't make sense, so maybe Abbot was crazy. He wasn't able to go out and face the town, and that was a hard fate for a man who had had as much power as he'd had.

Things began to happen later in the week. Maggie told me that Abbot had spent the afternoon with John Bains, the banker. Abbot still hadn't left the Golden Palace. He'd sent Maggie to fetch Bains.

She let me think that over, watching me to see how I was taking it, then she said: "He sold his ranch to Bains. He says he's leaving the country."

That stunned me. I didn't think he'd give up what he had here. I said: "He's taking it hard."

"It's his pride again," Maggie said. "He thinks folks in town know what happened and they're laughing at him. He's afraid to let them see him."

"He's beaten girls before," I said.

"Sure, but he never got himself a beating out of it," Maggie said. "I guess a lot of people knew about him, but they never said or thought much about it. I'm not even sure how much they knew, or how much the girls told their men. They were so glad to see him get what he did this time that they've told every man who's come here. By this time everybody in town must know, and I think Joe knows they know."

"Has he said any more about Pete Green?"

"Yeah, he's been drinking quite a bit, and that's what loosens his tongue," she said. "He says he's hated Green for a long time, and Green had no business staying here in Miles City. He also says Lucky is the only woman he ever loved, so I guess that's why he hates Green."

"Probably," I said, "but I don't believe that about his loving Lucky. I don't think he could love any woman."

"I don't, either," Maggie said angrily, "and, what's more, he don't know what loyalty is. I've run this house for him ever since he opened it, and now he tells me he wants Lucky to have my job."

"Don't worry," I said. "She won't take it."

"I don't care whether she takes it or not," Maggie snapped. "It's just that he tells me I do a rotten job and I'm a fat old bag and Lucky is beautiful and she's got a great build and she's hell on high red wheels in bed."

"Walk out on him," I said.

"I would if it wasn't for my girls," she said bitterly. "I know what loyalty is if he don't."

She had another surprise for me the next day. As soon as I walked into the Golden Palace, she said: "Abe Calder has been here all afternoon, and he's buying Joe's store."

"I'll be damned," I said. "He must mean it about leaving town."

"He means it, all right," Maggie said. "He'll be selling this place next."

"Buy it," I said. "I'll help you raise the money."

"Maybe I will if it comes to that," she said. "All I know is that he hasn't left his room all week, but he says he's going to tomorrow."

I didn't like to hear it, although I didn't figure he was going to stay inside the Golden Palace forever. It was just that I had hoped to put it off a while. I knew that when he showed up downtown, he'd open the ball in one way or another. I didn't know, either, whether he'd be after me for the first dance, or he'd be looking for Pete Green.

When I stepped into the Golden Palace early the next evening, Maggie said: "It was right peaceful today. Joe was even civil to me. He didn't say much, but when he left a few minutes ago, he said he was going to square everything up."

"Did you make an offer for this place?"

She nodded. "He wouldn't get down to cases. He put me off, saying we'd talk about it tomorrow."

I didn't see anything of him the first part of the evening as I made my rounds, but along toward eleven I dropped into Wolf's Saloon, and there was Joe Abbot, sitting at a table in the back of the room, his gaze on Lucky.

Abbot didn't move for about ten minutes except to fill his glass on the table in front of him. I moved along the bar until I was behind him, but I don't think he knew I was there. He simply didn't take his gaze off Lucky. He reminded me of a snake trying to hypnotize his prey.

I eased forward until I was only about two steps behind Abbot. I don't know why I did it, except that I figured he was up to something, but I couldn't guess what. It was just that he seldom went into Wolf's Saloon, and I didn't believe he'd be here now if he wasn't up to some meanness.

About twenty men were in the saloon: some were at the bar, some sitting at tables drinking, and the rest playing poker. Five men were at Green's table: John Bains, the banker; Eli Whitcomb, a lawyer; Doc Lewis; a drummer whose name I didn't know; and Pete Green, of course. Lucky, as usual, was standing behind Green, partly hidden by him from where Abbot sat.

I shot a glance at her, wondering if she knew Abbot was in the place. I brought my gaze back to Abbot immediately. Whatever he was going to do, he'd do fast, and I was afraid something might happen that would draw me away.

The notion came to me that he was here to shoot Green, and he couldn't do it as long as Green was sitting at the table with several other men. He'd probably wait until Green got to his feet for some reason.

I would have arrested Abbot and hauled him out of there if I could have thought of an excuse, but I couldn't jail him just for sitting there peaceful-like and staring at Lucky, so I was helpless until he made his move.

I heard Lucky sneeze. I didn't look at her, but I had the feeling she had stepped away from the table, maybe to wipe her nose. The move must have brought her fully into Abbot's view. At least, he decided he'd never have a better chance. He rose, his gun in his hand, and, before I could move, he fired directly at Lucky.

Hell broke loose with a bang. Lucky screamed and went down. I don't know if Abbot aimed to fire again or not. Anyhow, I was on him before he had time for another shot, my left hand grabbing his right hand and forcing it down.

The men at the poker table scattered and hit the floor. Then Green saw that Lucky was down, and he yelled: "She's bleeding, Doc. She's bleeding to death."

My first thought was to get Abbot out of there. At the moment, Pete Green didn't know who had fired the shot, but he'd hear soon enough, and he'd kill Abbot if he had the chance. I wrestled the gun out of Abbot's hand as I said: "Head for the door."

He didn't move soon enough to suit me, so I dug the muzzle of my gun into his backbone hard enough to loosen a couple of vertebræ. "Git, you son-of-a-bitch," I said. "Move."

He obeyed that time. I don't think Green even then knew who had fired the shot. I heard him call out in agony: "She's bleeding to death, Doc. My God, can't you stop it?"

I didn't want to be there if Lucky bled to death. I pushed Abbot through the batwings into the street, suddenly realizing my finger was squeezing the trigger. I had never hated a man so much in my life as I hated Joe Abbot at that moment. I wanted to see him dead, and nothing would have suited me better than for Green to have killed him, but it would have put Green into hot water, and I didn't want that to happen.

As soon as we were in the street, I moved back one step from Abbot. I said: "Run if you want to."

He didn't. He headed for the jail without being told. I locked him in the cell, then turned back and lighted a lamp. I picked it up and held it so the light fell into the cell. Abbot was sitting on a bunk, staring into space.

"You'll hang for this, if she dies," I said.

He didn't say anything. He didn't look at me. He just sat there, a dazed expression on his face. I don't think he knew where he was. I set the lamp down on my desk and blew it out, then left the jail.

Nothing about this made sense. Abbot certainly must have known he couldn't shoot Lucky and walk out of the saloon. Maybe he'd intended to shoot Pete Green, too, but he hadn't looked around to see if anyone was behind him. I decided he must have reached the place where he wasn't even thinking sense.

Chapter Fifteen

Lucky didn't die, although Sandy thought she would have been better off if she had. I didn't see her after the shooting while the wound healed. No one saw her except Doc Lewis and Sandy. I guess Pete Green saw all of her except her face, and she wouldn't let him see that. She had a bandage that covered most of her face, and, after the doctor cut down the size of the bandage, she wore a heavy black veil.

"She's going to have a terrible scar on the left side of her face," Sandy told me. "It even draws up the corner of her mouth. She doesn't want anybody to see her. She lies in bed and cries most of the day. She even talks about killing herself."

"Her beauty was her biggest asset," I said.

"Along with her ability to entertain a man in bed," Sandy agreed, "and her beauty helped that."

"She'll never stand behind Pete again while he plays poker," I said.

"That's part of what worries her," Sandy said. "The other thing that bothers her is that Pete will leave her because of the way she looks. It adds up to the same thing. She can't think of anything else except losing Pete."

"And she knows she can't find another man for a meal ticket now."

Sandy gave me a sharp, half-angry glance. "She'd have swapped Pete for you when you first came to Miles City, if you'd been willing, and then I'd never have got you."

"I think she would have," I said, "but I was interested in you."

Lucky refused to leave the cabin where she and Pete Green lived until after dark. Sandy bought her groceries and anything else she needed. It was a situation that couldn't go on indefinitely, and I wondered what would come of it.

I was surprised that Green didn't cuss Abbot and threaten to kill him, but he never said a word in my hearing. The shooting, of course, was the main topic of conversation around town for weeks. The fact that Lucky never made a public appearance afterward added to the speculation.

At first there was a good deal of talk about lynching Abbot. Most of the men in town knew Lucky, and the women had heard about her. I don't know if Abbot ever had had any real friends in Miles City, but, if he had, he lost them after the shooting.

A combination of what had happened in the Golden Palace and his attempt to take Lucky's life was enough to make him the most hated man in town. The tough element that supposedly looked to Abbot for leadership failed to make an appearance.

After John Bains bought Abbot's ranch, he made it clear that a man on the dodge wasn't welcome, and that helped get rid of some of the toughs who used to hang around Miles City. When I passed the word that any hanging party would lose the first five men who attempted a lynching, that kind of talk died down fast.

I still couldn't figure out Abbot. Most of the time he ate his meals and slept, or just lay on the bunk, staring at nothing. When I put other men in the cell, Abbot ignored them. He didn't say a word the first three days he was there. After that he didn't say much. That was why I was surprised when he asked one day about a week after the shooting how Lucky was getting along.

"She's alive," I said, "but I think she wishes she was dead.

What difference does it make to you? You tried to kill her."

"It makes a lot of difference to me," he said. "I didn't aim to kill her. I would have if that was what I intended to do. I love her. I just wanted to fix her so Green would throw her out. Has he done it yet?"

"No."

Abbot sighed. "She'll have a scarred face, won't she?"

"Yes."

"He won't go on living with her, will he?" Abbot asked.

"It's none of my business."

"You send word to her that as soon as I get out of here," Abbot said, "I'll take care of her."

"That's going to be a long time from now," I said. "They've got accommodations for you at Deer Lodge for about ten years."

All of this made about as much sense as the rest of the things Abbot had done lately. He had a pile of money in John Bains's bank. I don't know how much, but there was plenty of gossip about it around town.

One man who had been a teller in Bains's bank said it was over $50,000, but he may have been lying. It sounded like too much to me, but maybe not, because he'd had a good business as long as he'd been in Miles City.

On top of that, he had the money he'd received for his store and ranch. The man who told the story had quit working in the bank before Abbot had made those sales. I never heard what he got for his property, but the total now would be a hell of a lot more than $50,000 if that figure had been correct.

The point is that Abbot never mentioned this money, and apparently had forgotten he had it. I told him once he ought to send for a lawyer, and he said: "I can't afford one." Still, he must not have thought he was that poor, because he wouldn't talk to Maggie Adams about selling the Golden Palace.

Maggie came in several times and tried to make a deal. John Bains had changed his mind and had offered to lend Maggie all she needed, but Abbot just wouldn't listen. She tried to persuade him to sell, she pleaded, she begged, but he just lay on his bunk and acted as if he didn't hear a word.

I had trouble making up my mind whether Abbot was crazy or not, but one thing was sure. He was able to close his mind to any thought he didn't like, just as he was able to close his ears to words he didn't want to hear. Apparently he lived in a strange world where everything was perfect for Joe Abbot.

One day he asked me when he was coming up for trial. I said: "I don't know. It'll be whenever the judge gets here from Helena. You ought to be glad you're still here. They tell me Deer Lodge is a hell of a place to live."

"Oh, I won't go there," he said cheerfully. "They'll acquit me, and I'll put Lucky in charge of the Golden Palace. Everything will be like it used to be."

I decided then he was crazy. At least, he wasn't living in the same world I was.

One thing I was curious about was why he wasn't sore at me, so I asked him.

He seemed surprised. He looked at me blankly, then he said: "I never wasted any love on you, and I wanted to fire you, but that makes me no never-mind now. You were doing what you thought was your duty, but it's different with that son-of-a-bitch of a Pete Green. He's the only man I ever hated, and Lucky is the only woman I ever loved."

I let it go at that, but it seemed to me he had a wonderful talent for twisting facts to suit his own pleasure. I suppose that was proof enough of his insanity. I'm convinced that the beating I gave him with the strap was what made him go the way he did. He could not face himself or the town.

Still, it seemed strange to me that he didn't kill Green when he had a chance, if he hated the gambler so much. Then he could have offered to take care of Lucky. That would have been logical, but there I go, forgetting that the logic of my world had nothing to do with the way Joe Abbot thought and acted.

A much more rational question was why Green had not reacted more violently than he had to Abbot's attempt to kill Lucky. His casual indifference was not in keeping with his character. I should have been tipped off when Sandy said one night: "Did you know that Pete Green is broke?"

"No, I didn't know that," I said. "How'd you hear?"

"Lucky told me," Sandy answered. "It seems that Pete hasn't had any luck since she was shot. Not any big luck, like a gambler needs. It's been a steady erosion of his capital. Now she says they're leaving Miles City and they'll camp out. Just live off the country for a while."

"The hell," I said.

I couldn't believe it. Pete Green had been an institution in Miles City ever since I had been there, and long before, and Lucky had been part of the institution.

I never had understood luck the way a gambler does. It's a matter of being sensitive to it, I suppose, knowing when to keep on playing and when to quit. After Lucky was shot and could no longer stand behind Pete Green, he must have lost that intuitive touch. Anyhow, since Lucky was able to travel, they sold the things they couldn't take, and they were going to ride out of town on two horses with a blanket roll tied behind each saddle.

I thought about it the next morning and decided that Green must be as crazy as Joe Abbot. I just couldn't figure them leaving Miles City that way, broke, and headed God knows where. Lucky wasn't the kind of woman to rough it, and I thought Pete Green was too much of a dandy even to attempt it.

As I said, I should have figured things out, but I didn't sense what was happening, even after I got to the jail that noon and found Lucky sitting astride a horse and holding the reins of a second animal.

I said: "I hear you're leaving town."

Lucky had that heavy black veil over her face, so I couldn't see what she looked like. I was satisfied for it to be that way. Sandy said the scar made her look hideous, and I was happy to remember her the way I had known her.

She said in a normal, friendly voice: "That's right. We're going on a vacation. Pete's never camped out much, and we thought it would be. . . ."

A gun went off inside the jail. I wheeled toward the front door and took one long stride toward it, then stopped. Lucky had fired at my feet. I heard the gun go off behind me, and I saw the little geyser of dust that the bullet kicked up in front of me. I swung around. Lucky was pointing a .32 at me.

"I hope I won't have to kill you, Marshal," Lucky said. Her tone was not all friendly now. "I will, if you make any wrong moves. Freeze right where you are."

I thought I knew Lucky pretty well, but I suddenly decided I didn't know her at all. I'm convinced she would have killed me if I'd reached for my gun, so I did the smart thing. I froze.

Pete Green ran out of the jail, shouting at me: "Drop your gun belt, Dave."

People who had heard the shots were moving toward the jail to see what had happened. I sensed I was standing close to death from Pete as well as Lucky, so I didn't waste any time dropping my gun belt. Green scooped it up and stepped into the saddle, saying: "Stay right there, Dave. You go after a gun, and you're dead."

They went down Main Street, churning up the dust, and headed downstream. I waited a few seconds, then bolted for the jail door. Bill Dillon was lying on the floor, out cold. I grabbed a .30-30 from the gun rack and ran outside, remembering that Lucky had said once: "You owe Pete one life."

I could have knocked Green out of his saddle, but I didn't. I shot high, and, as soon as they were out of range, I put the rifle down. I yelled at one of the men: "Get Doc Lewis!"

When I got back inside the jail, Bill Dillon was sitting up. He said: "That damned Green suckered me into being careless. He claimed he wanted to see you. When I told him you hadn't come in, he said he'd wait. I turned my back, and that was when the roof caved in."

I went on past Dillon to the cell. Abbot was lying on the floor, a bullet hole between his eyes. I turned around and walked back to the office. Doc Lewis was there, feeling Dillon's head. Abe Calder and John Bains had come in, and others were crowding into the room.

"Pete Green shot and killed Joe Abbot," I said.

"Good," John Bains said. "I hope none of you star-toters go after him. He ought to have a medal for shooting Joe Abbot, not a hang rope."

From the way the others nodded agreement, it struck me that Bains expressed what everybody thought. As for me, going after Pete was the last thing I wanted to do.

Chapter Sixteen

We didn't hear anything of Pete Green and Lucky for a long time. I assumed that they had gone to Bismarck or Deadwood or maybe Cheyenne, and Pete would go on gambling. Still, men were coming to Miles City from those towns, and I often asked about Pete, but none knew him or had even heard of him.

He may have changed his name, thinking the law would come after him for killing Abbot, but I didn't want him. The sheriff said blandly: "Sure I want him, but I don't know where to look for him." The trouble was, Pete didn't know this, so he and Lucky may have kept on running.

Late in the afternoon of the day Abbot was killed, someone had picked up my gun and belt where Green had tossed them to one side of the street. I was glad to get them back. I'd been afraid Pete had kept them.

Abbot's funeral drew the smallest number of mourners of any funeral I ever went to. I was there, along with Maggie and her girls, the undertaker, and the preacher. I went because I felt a little guilty for setting into motion the series of events that had led to his death. Maggie and her girls went because he had been their employer and so felt an obligation. The preacher went because he had to, and the undertaker was there because it was his job. It all added up to the fact that Joe Abbot had died as friendless as a man could.

Miles City settled down to an even level of life. A good deal of building went on, including the McQueen House, known originally as the Interocean Hotel. It wasn't anything great compared to what a man would find in a bigger city, but for Miles City it was great.

For the first time we had decent hotel accommodations. The rooms were not large, and the walls were so thin that a person in one room could hear what went on in another room next door, an embarrassing situation for female visitors from the East.

We also had Russell's skating rink, which served as an arena for wrestling matches and as a hall for conventions. The First National Bank was the first brick building in town. I was told that bricks cost seventy-five cents each. The result was we had few brick buildings. The craftsmen who made the decorations on the false fronts on the business buildings received seven dollars a day, so they were an independent lot who worked only when they felt like it.

The red-light district grew with new buildings. A madam came from Deadwood and bought the house next to the Golden Palace and refurbished it so it had more glitter and shine than the Palace. She brought in new girls from Cheyenne and Denver, a better class of hookers for the cowboy trade, which was greater than ever. Joe Abbot had prophesied this would happen the day I was hired.

We had Cowboy Annie and Connie and Cowboy Queen and others of about that quality. We also had a number of variety houses, and the girls who worked in them lived in small cottages that were conveniently located just behind the theaters. The regular hookers felt this was unfair competition.

We had more families, which meant more *good women,* more churches, and more schools. I suppose this was progress. There was less shooting in the streets, fewer drunks lying in the gutter, and a greater clamor for law and order.

In one way this was good, but I liked the flexibility of a pioneer society, and I began to feel boxed in. Not that I gave a thought to leaving Miles City. Sandy was happy here. I was happy, and my lots were becoming more valuable every day.

One thing happened that fall which illustrates my point. A wealthy Englishman named Reginald Tobias arrived in town with his wife, an American woman in her late twenties and a beauty. I suspect that her mere presence with her fine clothes and expensive perfume made the *good women* jealous. They made it a point to ignore her. She was without female friends, a fact that did not bother her in the least.

One morning a rancher returned to his room in the McQueen House after breakfast. When he passed Mrs. Tobias's room, the door was open, and she was standing in front of her mirror admiring herself with nothing on except her rings and a pearl necklace. She had, the rancher said, "the purtiest figure he ever saw on a female human critter," and he stopped to admire it. He said she acted as if she didn't know he was watching.

The story was told in all of the saloons in Miles City, and I think that every time she appeared on the street in her fashionable dresses and plumed hats and pink parasols, the men who saw her wished they'd been the rancher who had seen her with nothing on, and began picturing what she looked like clad only in her rings and pearl necklace.

The Tobiases were in Miles City a month or more. He had all the money in the world, judging from the way he acted. They lived a very sedate life, without a breath of scandal, unless what the rancher saw that morning constituted a scandal.

They rented a buggy nearly every day to ride out to some of the nearby ranches, Tobias wanting to buy one if he found an outfit that he liked. Mrs. Tobias spent a good deal of Mr. Tobias's money in the Miles City stores. They ate their meals in the McQueen House.

Everything was fine until one day the madam who had moved in beside the Golden Palace was downtown making a deposit in the First National Bank and spotted Mrs. Tobias on the street. She recognized her as a famous chippy from Chicago. Of course, she told some of her men customers, and the story eventually reached the *good women*.

The next thing I knew, I had a delegation visit me consisting of preachers and *good women*. They insisted that I run Mrs. Tobias out of town. I refused, saying it was none of my business. They kept pushing me, so I finally agreed to mention it to Mr. and Mrs. Tobias, but I refused to put any pressure on them. I did mention it, and the Tobiases took the next train out of town, much to the regret of the local merchants.

It was, I guess, a sign that Miles City was growing up, but I liked it the old way, when no one in town would have given a damn one way or the other about Mrs. Tobias.

The hide hunters were back that winter. We had, or so I was told, 2,200 people in town, and I believed it. That, of course, did not include the soldiers and their people at the fort. Wood cost seven dollars a cord; coal was the same for a ton.

The county built a three-story brick courthouse, which was our pride and joy, even though a good many taxpayers threw up their hands in horror and said it would bankrupt us. We even had a barber who claimed he was a "capillary manipulation boss barber and hairdresser." Yes, indeed, Miles City was growing up.

My relationship with Sandy was almost perfect. We often went hunting up the Tongue River when she had time, and we nearly always brought back some prairie chickens or sage hens, and occasionally a deer. I ate most of my suppers with her, and I'm sure it was common knowledge in Miles City that Sandy was my girl, but I don't think many people knew I was sleeping with her.

One thing did irk me. We had no social life together. If I

was invited to someone's home for Sunday dinner, I was considered a bachelor, and I usually was asked because there was an available young woman in the home who more likely than not would be as ugly as sin. I didn't go around telling it, but the truth was, there was not a woman in the world who could have taken me from Sandy.

I found this situation particularly true at the fort. I became acquainted with a number of officers who were married and had their families at the fort. I was invited quite often into their homes, sometimes to take part in a sport they had going, sometimes to listen to a band concert, or to go to a dance.

During the long Montana winters the officers and their wives had to struggle to find things to do for entertainment, so they came up with ideas such as flooding the parade ground and using it for a skating rink, or simply going on sleigh rides. I nearly always accepted these invitations and was grateful for them. I liked the Army people and enjoyed being with them, but I resented the fact that Sandy was always ignored. In many ways the town was dependent on the fort, so it was simply good business to go, and men like John Bains and Abe Calder encouraged me to accept all the invitations I received. Still, as I say, I resented the situation, and I couldn't help blowing off to Sandy about it.

One of the things I admired most about Sandy was her ability to accept disappointments and not get upset by them. She would nod and smile and say: "I'd like to go with you, Dave, just as much as you want me to go, but it's impossible, so if it's important to you, you've simply got to find a woman who does not live in the twilight zone."

"It isn't that important," I said.

I knew she was right, and I doubted if anything would have been changed if we were married. I nagged her about getting a divorce, but she put it off for one reason or another until I finally realized she had moral or religious scruples about divorce, so I quit talking about it, glad that we had at least a friendship that was nearly as good as marriage.

Sandy missed Lucky. It was true that she visited with the girls from the Golden Palace, but it was not the same as it had been with Lucky, who had been her personal friend. Sometimes she'd say: "I worry about her, Dave. She never had much self-confidence, and, after she was shot, she had less. I just don't know what will happen to her."

"What you mean is that Pete may leave her," I said.

Sandy nodded. "To me he's not a likable man. He's too cold, but Lucky loved him in her own way, and she certainly depended on him."

I didn't have time to worry about Lucky, but I did think about her and Pete Green, and wonder what happened to them. Then, late in the following spring, we heard, and we were all shocked by what we heard.

The Deadwood stage came in going hell-for-leather one afternoon, the driver wounded and the guard dead, shot through the head. The two passengers were not hurt beyond being robbed and scared half to death.

" 'Bout ten miles out," the driver told us, "they got the strongbox and robbed the passengers, but I don't know how much they lost. Four were in the gang, three men and one woman. The woman wore a heavy black veil and a tan duster. The men were masked, but I knew the bastard who shot me and killed the guard. I played cards at his table in Wolf's Saloon too many times not to recognize Pete Green's voice."

At first I didn't believe it, but I questioned both passengers. Their description of the outlaw leader fitted Pete Green as far as size and build went, and what they said about the woman fitted Lucky just as well.

The sheriff led a posse after them, but the outlaws were

out of the country by that time and skillfully hid their tracks so that the sheriff lost the trail within a mile or so of the scene of the hold-up.

I told Sandy, and she accepted it without batting an eye. She said: "Lucky would go along with anything Pete did. He probably thinks he's wanted for murder, so he doesn't figure that one or a dozen killings will make any difference for him."

I was disappointed and a little sick. I could respect a gambler; I could not in any way respect a road agent who was a killer, and I wanted to respect Pete. From what the driver and the passengers said, there was no excuse for killing the guard.

One thing I did know. My debt to Pete Green had been paid in full.

Chapter Seventeen

Change came to Miles City in the following months. It wasn't due to Joe Abbot's death or the fact that Pete Green and Lucky had left town, or to any of my personal efforts. The change was foreordained; the handwriting had been on the wall, but few men had read it as plainly as Jeff Munro.

The buffalo were killed off. To all intents and purposes, the northern herd had been wiped out, although several years passed before the last buffalo was killed in Montana. Those of us who had seen the great herds were fortunate because we had been in the right place at the right time to witness a phenomenon of the West. It was incredible that the great animals had ever existed in such staggering numbers. Now they were gone, and they would never return.

The hide hunters, too, were gone. No one mourned their passing, but they had brought a period of boom prosperity to Miles City, and now the merchants and saloonkeepers were forced to settle down to a more even flow of business. A few of the hunters turned to ranching, and some found work in town, but for the most part they simply disappeared the way geese go south in the fall.

Another change was the fact that the riverboats almost stopped running, now that the railroad had come to Miles City. In a way I hated to see the boats stop. It was always exciting in the spring to wait for the breakup on the Yellowstone and then the high water and the arrival of the first boat, probably in June. Somehow the clanging of bells and the whoosh of steam and the whistle of locomotives never quite made up for the loss of excitement that the riverboats had given us.

The woodcutters disappeared just as the hide hunters did. This, too, brought a loss of revenue to the merchants and saloons. I don't know how many woodcutting camps had made their living cutting wood for the river steamers, but the number had been considerable, and most of them had bought their supplies in Miles City. Too, they came to town to raise hell and blow their money when the river went down and boats stopped running in late summer or early fall.

There was the other side of the coin, of course. Miles City had become a railroad town, but more than that it was a cow town. As the herds continued to come in from Texas and Oregon, and as the number of ranches increased, the number of cowboys increased. The interesting thing to me was that for a time after Joe Abbot's death the violence in town decreased, a sort of lull before the storm, and then it broke loose in a bigger whoop-de-do than ever. Hardly a night passed that Bill Dillon and I didn't have a dozen cowhands in jail.

But there was a difference. Most of the trouble the cowboys caused was from rowdyism and sheer animal spirits and what they considered good-natured fun. They were interesting men, seldom mean, and always exciting and unpredictable. There was a question of where fun stopped and trouble began, a judgment that Dillon and I had to make every day. On occasion we simply looked in the opposite direction, but there were other times when we had to take a hand, times when the cowboy's idea of a practical joke went too far.

One day a new girl working at the Golden Palace went out through the back door to go the privy. Her name was Sadie Grogan. She was on the fat side, probably the least exciting girl that Maggie Adams had and one that Maggie wouldn't have taken on if she could have done better, but there were other houses in Miles City by this time that were as high class as the Golden Palace, and Maggie discovered that she had to do with what she could get.

A cowboy was waiting outside, but whether he was waiting for Sadie is something I never found out. Maybe he would have done the same with any other girl, but I always suspected that several cowboys thought up this caper and that it was a put-up job to get rid of Sadie. Anyhow, as soon as she got inside and closed the door and had time to sit down, he threw his rope over the privy, jerked it off its foundation, and hauled it down the alley for about fifty yards.

I guess she thought it was an earthquake. You never heard such caterwauling in your life. I heard her a block away and started for the alley on the run. Maggie went out the back door with her shotgun and let go a blast, but she was too far away to do any good.

The cowboy was gone before I got there, and I never did find out who he was, but the dust hadn't settled in the alley when I reached the privy. I opened the door and pulled Sadie out. She wasn't hurt except for some bruises, but her sense of dignity was completely destroyed.

I got on one side and Maggie got on the other, and we practically carried her into the Golden Palace. She was complaining something fierce all the way, bawling and cussing and acting like she was clean out of her mind. She caught the next train out of town, and we never heard of her again.

I told Sandy about it that night. I thought it was funny, and I guess every man in town did, too, but not Sandy. She said: "Dave, that girl could have been killed."

"Not likely," I said, "but she sure got a shaking up." I laughed, and added: "I wonder if she ever got her job done."

"I think it was a shameful thing," Sandy said, "but I've got a hunch that Sadie brought it on herself. I'll never know, and Maggie won't say if she ever finds out, but I'll bet the other girls put the cowboy up to that stunt. Sadie was a bitchy woman, and they all hated her. They played every trick on her that you could think of, but she wouldn't leave. Chances are they cooked this up to get her out of the Palace."

"It worked," I said.

Sandy snorted. "Murder works, too, but it's not a good way to get rid of someone."

That same winter one of the variety houses had a program that included a huge woman who claimed to be a soprano. She could hit the high notes, all right, but for me I'd rather listen to a cow bawl, and I guess the boys felt the same way. Anyhow, one night while she was in the middle of holding a high note, three cowboys who occupied a box almost directly above her dropped a rope over her and pulled her up into the box.

I wasn't there, but from the way I heard it, the soprano used some words that were enough to teach the cowhands a lesson in profanity. It must have been a sight, seeing that woman, who was about as shapely as a cow and weighed nearly as much, being hoisted all the way up into that box, kicking and bellowing like a stuck hog until they hauled her over the edge.

As soon as she got into the box, she lit into those three cowhands. I guess they thought they'd caught a she-lion, and they got her out of there *pronto*. Somebody came after me. By the time I got there, she was lying on her back, claiming it was broken and she was dying, and she ordered me to find those cowboys and hang all three of them.

They were identified by the man who ran the variety house, so I started looking for them, not being in too much of a hurry. They had time to get out of town, which was the way I wanted it. When they showed up again, the woman was gone, and everybody else was glad to forget the whole business, which was also the way I wanted it.

The funniest thing that happened, and the story that was told all over Montana, had to do with a young Texas cowboy named Bud Miller. He'd been around town a year or more, and I knew him pretty well. He was little and feisty and had more guts for his size than any other man in Miles City.

He was too proddy to suit me. He'd tackle a man if he got mad, regardless of size, and more often than not he'd handle the big bruisers, who would swear afterward that they'd been fighting a buzz saw, not a man. Once in a while Bud would run into somebody he couldn't lick, or he'd take on two men at a time, and I'd have to break up the fight or he'd have got badly hurt.

I had Bud in jail a dozen times that first year he was around Miles City. Every time I let him out, he'd swear he was going to stay out of trouble, but he never kept his promise. As soon as he got a couple of drinks under his belt, he'd start looking for a fight.

He fell in love with Rosebud, and she fell just as hard. That surprised me. She was a busy girl, the most popular one in the Golden Palace. I didn't think she'd ever fall for a man, but Bud was just right for her. They sure made a pair. One time she bet him he wouldn't put on one of her floppy, plumed hats and a pair of her purple bloomers and ride down Main Street. He wasn't a man to be backed down on a bet, so he did it. That ride was the talk of the town for a month.

The funny thing I mentioned wasn't funny to Maggie Adams. It happened in the fall of 1883. Bud and a couple of other cowhands were hanging around the Golden Palace, talking to the girls. They weren't there for business, and they weren't drinking, so after a while Maggie had enough of it and told them to get out.

Of course, they couldn't hear her. Bud sat down at the piano and started beating out a tune, making more noise than rhythm. Maggie told them again to leave, but Bud yelled back that he couldn't hear her. She got her mouth right down to his ear and bellowed: "Get out of here!"

"All right," he said, "but I'll be back."

In a few minutes he was back, this time riding his horse. He rode that animal right through the front door into the parlor. The first thing the horse did was to make a deposit on Maggie's new, expensive rug. She always claimed he had that horse trained to wait until he was standing on the rug.

That was enough for Maggie. She ran out of the house, looking for me. As soon as Bud saw me coming, he rode out of the house by way of the bay window, showering glass around for fifty feet. I yelled at him to stop, but he just dug in the steel and headed for the ferry.

I couldn't run as fast as Bud's horse, but I made a good try, shooting over his head every minute or two. When Bud reached the river, the ferry was several feet from the bank, but he didn't stop or even hesitate. He put that horse through the air in the longest jump I ever saw, barely catching the edge of the ferry, then he turned around in the saddle and thumbed his nose at me.

The next time Bud came to town, Maggie was over her mad and she wouldn't press charges. Maybe Rosebud paid for the rug, but Maggie never got a new one, as far as I know. The last time I was in the Golden Palace, that spot was still there.

As far as the town was concerned, Dillon and I kept the lid on pretty well, not too tightly, but tightly enough so that a woman could walk along Main Street and be perfectly safe. There was a good deal of social life: box socials, dramatics, band concerts, musicals, ice-cream socials, and sleighing parties in the winter. The solid citizens of Miles City took part in these activities, the respectable women never really knowing much about what went on in the red-light district or the sa-loons.

I didn't realize for a long time how bad conditions were in the county. The town was my responsibility, but the county was a different proposition. It was so big that the sheriff simply couldn't handle the lawlessness. Even with the number of people who had moved into eastern Montana in the last two or three years, there were still large areas where no one lived except transients who lived off the country, or outlaws who were getting better organized all the time.

I didn't think much about the outlaw activity until Jeff Munro drove a herd into Miles City that fall to ship. When I heard that Jeff was loading, I went down to the pens and watched. It was a hell of a mess, dust and cow manure and sweat, cattle bawling, and men cursing and yelling orders and sometimes howling in pain. Accidents did happen, and Doc Lewis was kept busy.

As soon as Munro saw me, he came to where I was standing and held out his hand. "I'm glad to see you, Dave," he said.

It was the most sincere greeting I ever heard, and it gave me pleasure. To my way of thinking, Jeff Munro was a great man. I respected him and liked him, and I was proud to be his friend. I'd never felt quite the same about any other man. I'd have gone to hell and back if he'd asked me, and in the end that was just about what I did.

"I'm glad to see you, Jeff," I said. "You're loading some good-looking beef. I guess you'll be rich when you get to Chicago."

"Rich?" He glared at me, his eyes bloodshot from the dust. He poked me in the chest with a forefinger. "I want to talk to you, Dave. I'll buy you a drink and a supper tonight at the McQueen House after I get cleaned up."

"It's the best offer I've had today," I said. "I'll take it."

I was waiting for him when he came down the stairs into the lobby, shaved and bathed and wearing a clean shirt and smelling of bay rum. He didn't tell me what was on his mind until after we were sitting in the dining room and had given our orders to the waitress, then he leaned forward and took his cigar out of his mouth.

"Dave," he said, "I'm in a hell of a lot of trouble. So's every other stockman in eastern Montana. You used to wonder where all the hardcases went after Joe Abbot was killed. Well, I'll tell you. They're hiding out in the old wood camps along the Missouri and the Yellowstone, and they're stealing us blind. If we don't clean 'em out in the next year, we'll be broke."

I was shocked. Sure, I'd heard stories of cattle rustling and horse stealing, and I knew some outlaws had holed up in the badlands along the river, but this was strong talk. If it had been from some other man, I would have discounted it, but not from Jeff Munro.

"Cattle?" I asked.

He nodded. "But mostly it's horses, and what kind of a cattle outfit have you got when you lose your horses? These devils are organized. That's the trouble. The run 'em into Canada and sell 'em, then they steal more horses and sell 'em back to ranchers in Montana and the Dakotas."

I didn't know what to say. I ate for a minute, thinking about it, then I said: "There's not much I can do about it, Jeff. Not here in Miles City. If there is something. . . ."

"There is, Dave," he said. "Not just now, I reckon, but there'll be a day."

That was all he'd say. It was spring before I knew what he had in mind.

Chapter Eighteen

I heard a lot more about the outlaws that fall before shipping time was over. All of the ranchers were scared. The long riders were organized, the stockmen said. They had spies out. They knew when and where the sheriff and his posse would be at any given time, and they were always somewhere else. Some smart bastard had got them together.

A few small ranchers were in cahoots with the outlaws, or so the talk said. Some of the little storekeepers, too. There were a number of these small stores all over eastern Montana, just a few staples on the shelves and usually a post office in one corner. The point was, the owners could play innocent and still be a big help to the outlaws if they were of a mind to do it.

The newspapers built the fire a little higher with scare stories about the outlaws. Men in the saloons gathered along the bars and agreed that a few necktie parties would clear the air. The merchants in Miles City got boogery, knowing they'd go broke if the cowmen did. Most of the ranchers bought their supplies on the cuff, and they'd pay up once a year after they shipped. If they didn't ship, they didn't pay. It was that simple.

Just before winter clamped down, the Deadwood stage was held up about twenty miles out of Miles City. The guard was killed, along with one passenger, a well-known cowman who had a spread up the Rosebud. He'd driven a herd to the Black Hills and was bringing the money back in gold, which he was carrying.

Someone had passed the word to the outlaws because they

didn't bother with anyone else or even take the strongbox. All they wanted was the rancher's gold. He tried to draw his gun, but they cut him down, then rode away with his gold.

Again the driver identified the boss outlaw as Pete Green. "I tell you, I knew his voice," he insisted. "I played poker too long at his table to make a mistake."

The woman was again with the road agents. She wore the long tan duster and a heavy veil over her face, just as she had before. There were two other men, but the driver had no idea who they were. All he was sure of, he said, was that Green had done the killing.

The sheriff started out with a posse that evening, and came back two days later with nothing. The wind had kicked the dust around so that the posse lost the trail after a few miles, but apparently the outlaws had crossed the Yellowstone near the mouth of the Powder River and simply disappeared into the maze of gullies and brush and cottonwoods.

Pete Green had gone a long ways down, and sooner or later he was going to stretch rope. He had written it in the book. I didn't waste any sympathy on him, but I did on Lucky. On the other hand, Sandy had no patience with her, and, when we talked about it, we always wound up in an argument.

"You say Pete brought all this on himself," she said, "and, when he's hanged, it's the same as committing suicide. He knows what he's doing. Well, I say it's the same with Lucky. She's no fool. She knows what she's doing, and she knows what will happen to her. I say that, if she goes along with Pete and helps hold up stages, then she's as responsible for the killings as the other two men, and she ought to hang right beside them."

I couldn't really argue against what she said, but I couldn't stand the prospect of Lucky's hanging along with the men. I still had some sympathy for her. She used to worry about being deserted. I was willing to bet she still worried about it, and that was why she went along with anything Pete did.

Winter clamped down on us, and we had a foot of snow on the ground before we knew it. Miles City life got pretty monotonous except for the hearty ones who liked to ice-skate or toboggan or go sleigh riding.

A good many ranchers spent the winter in the McQueen House. The talk went on around the potbellied stoves in the saloons and stores whether any ranchers were on hand or not, and the main topic of conversation was always organization.

"The stockmen have got to organize," John Bains said. "That's where the outlaws have had the advantage. There's got to be a Territorial Stockgrowers' Association. If they co-operated, they could catch and hang every one of the thieving bastards."

Doc Lewis and Abe Calder and the rest of the Miles City merchants agreed. I'm sure there was quite a bit of writing going on. Before spring it was set. The first annual meeting of the Territorial Stockgrowers' Association was called to order in Miles City on April 21st.

The meeting was held in the roller-skating rink on Eighth and Pleasant Streets. The weather was wintry, but the ranchers came from all over Montana, the big ones like Jeff Munro and Conrad Kohrs and Pierre Wibaux, along with dozens of small ones. We even had Theodore Roosevelt and the Marquis de Mores from the Little Missouri on the other side of the Dakota line.

Every bedroom in Miles City was filled. Most of the wives came, too. The first thing that Jeff Munro did was to look me up. He said: "I know you're going to be busy with all these people in town, but I want you to attend the meetings of the association, no matter what happens."

"I'm no stockman," I said. "They won't let me in."

"I'll see that they do," he said. "Well, maybe it ain't important that you attend all the sessions we'll have. Some of the first will be damned dry until we get organized, but I want you to be there when the horse stealing comes up, which it sure as hell will. We wouldn't be organizing if it wasn't for that."

"All right," I said. "I don't know why you want me to come, but I'll be there if I know when."

"I'll see you get the word," he said.

I really didn't have any more to do than usual. The cowmen were older than the average cowboys, they were married with a few exceptions, and about all they did outside of the convention was to take a few drinks and play a few hands of poker.

The sessions were dry, just as Munro had said. I'd drop in and listen a few minutes, then leave. They elected officers, and Jeff Munro, as could have been expected, was elected president. Then they drew up their constitution and bylaws. They wrangled about who was eligible and what constituted a stockman. It was plain they were afraid of homesteaders, who were bound to hit Montana like a plague of locusts sooner or later, and these men didn't want a homesteader who owned two cows to be called a stockman.

The last order of business was the discussion of how to handle the growing outlaw problem. The sheriff left town that morning, thinking, I guess, that he was going to be under fire. Munro got me up early, banging on my door and yelling: "Time to rise and shine, Dave! This is the day!"

I got to the hall just as Munro was pounding his gavel for order. About five minutes later the whole outfit seemed to blow up. The outlaw problem had brought them here. They had waited patiently through all of the boring preliminary business of getting organized, and now the dam broke.

I had a feeling that every man there wanted to speak at once. It took Munro several minutes to restore order. When he did, he promised them they would all get a chance to speak, and began by recognizing a rancher from the upper Rosebud named Bert Yancey.

He made a rousing five-minute speech, saying that outlawry more than anything else would hold back the development of the West, and the only way to stop it was to hang the horse thieves. He ended up by offering to lead a column of cowboys to wipe out the horse thieves, then challenged other ranchers to do the same.

Roosevelt and the marquis called for action. Others who spoke said much the same thing. The law officers weren't condemned, but they received small praise. I had no idea whether a majority held this view or not, because the men who spoke were far less than a majority. When the verbal members had their say, Munro pointed his gavel at the crowd.

"Gentlemen," he said, "I doubt that any of you have been hurt any more than I have in the past year by the outlaws. I want them destroyed as much as anyone else, but we can't appoint ourselves law officers and lead unofficial posses after these men. In the first place, some honest men would be hurt. In the second place, we'd be making lawbreakers out of ourselves. In the third place, there is nothing we could do which would destroy public trust in us as quickly as the lawless action which you propose."

A strange, growling rumble rose from the crowd. Munro paused just a moment, then he said: "Gentlemen, let me remind you that I speak from experience. I am not ashamed of the action I took at Virginia City, but that was twenty years ago. Conditions have changed. We had no choice then. We do now. I promise you that steps will be taken to cut this cancerous growth from our industry." He cracked the desk with his gavel, then said: "I declare the first annual convention of the Territorial Stockgrowers' Association adjourned."

I didn't like the sound of the rumble from the crowd, which was coming on strong now. I was the first one down the aisle to the steps at the edge of the platform. Munro hesitated, his eyes sweeping the crowd. The men were on their feet, motionless for the moment, and I had a terrible feeling that if someone took the lead and said—"Let's get Munro!"—that I'd have a sudden problem on my hands.

"Jeff, for God's sake, get out of here," I said.

He swung toward me, nodding. "I guess I've done all I can."

He stepped down off the platform and left the building through the back door. I followed, keeping an eye on the crowd until I was outside. No one made a move to follow, maybe no one would have, but the crowd was unpredictable, and I'll admit that Munro's action in adjourning the meeting was peremptory to say the least.

Once we were outside in the wintry sunshine, he took a long breath and said: "Quite a meeting, wasn't it?"

"Yeah, it was, and not exactly what I expected out of you," I said.

A wry grin touched the corners of his mouth. "No, I guess not. Do you know why I wanted you to be there?"

"No."

"I wanted you to see first hand just what the members wanted and how they felt. Was there any doubt in your mind what would have been their decision if it had been put to a vote?"

"Well, yes," I said. "Some of them wanted to make a move, all right, but there are always some gabby men in that big a crowd. I don't know what the majority thought. A lot of them never opened their mouths."

He nodded. "That's right, but I was afraid to let it come to a vote. The fact remains that we have to do something. A few of us want to talk to you this morning. How about eight o'clock in the jail office? Is the jail empty? I don't want anyone overhearing us."

"It's empty, and no one will hear us," I said. "I'll be there unless something happens between now and then that keeps me from it."

"Good," he said, and walked away toward the McQueen House.

I watched this, not certain what he had in mind, but not liking what I guessed it was.

Chapter Nineteen

I was waiting in my office when they got there. Besides Munro, there were the Dunn twins and a fourth man I didn't know. Munro introduced him as Jerry Bowers from the upper river. I knew the Dunn boys. They were about my age and looked so much alike that I often wondered if their wives could tell them apart. Finally, to cut down the confusion, Ben had grown a black, bristly mustache and Sam remained clean-shaven.

The Dunns ran a horse ranch about twenty miles from town on the river. I knew they had been hard hit by the horse thieves in the last year or so, but they weren't the chronic gripers who hung around the Miles City saloons and cried from fear more than any real loss. The Dunns were six-footers, barrel-chested men, and, as I shook hands with them, I remembered that not once since I had been marshal here had I had the least trouble with either of them or any of their hands.

Bowers was older, about Munro's age. He had some of Munro's qualities, a natural aptitude for leadership, which is something you don't see but you feel, and I felt it in Bowers the same as I had the first time I met Jeff Munro.

"You boys are missing the big shindig in the McQueen House," I said.

"They can have a ball without us," Munro said a little sharply. "I ain't sure they'd want me there, anyhow."

Bowers shook his head. "You're dead wrong on that, Jeff. I wish you had let it come to a vote. I don't think we'd have passed any vigilante resolution."

"I don't, either," Sam Dunn said. "There's always some

136

loudmouths in a crowd, and they're the ones we were hearing."

"Sit down," I said, pointing to the chairs along the wall. "Let's get to whatever this committee has on its mind."

I sat there in my swivel chair behind the desk and waited. Munro cleared his throat, glanced at the three men who had come with him, and jumped in. "Dave, I didn't risk a vote on the vigilante business, but that's exactly what we've got to do, and it's what we're going to do. We don't have time to wait for the law to do the job, and I ain't sure it can until we have more people and more counties, so a sheriff don't have the whole outdoors to look after.

"If we had passed a resolution to take vigilante action, what we're going to do would be official. That was something we had to avoid at all costs. I want it understood that what we say is not to be repeated outside of this room. Our action will not represent the Stockholders' Association, but it is necessary to save the cattle business. A dozen men will be involved. To talk would put a noose on our necks, so I'm confident no one will know who's involved except us. Agreed?"

I nodded, but I didn't believe it. I didn't think you could get a dozen men together that didn't have at least one gabber among them. With public opinion what it was in Montana, I didn't think any official action would be taken, no matter how many horse thieves were hanged.

I didn't say it, though. Munro wasn't a man to argue with. Besides, he hadn't said what the plan was, or whether I'd be among the dozen, although I knew damned well I would be. I wasn't sure right then whether I would go along or not.

I'd been guessing along this line. I agreed with what Munro had said in the afternoon, that back in the Alder Gulch days there had been no choice, but there was now. Maybe my feeling came from wearing the star as long as I had. I didn't use to think that way. I realized that I had come to look at the law in a different way than I did before I became a lawman.

In the long run, the law and honest law-enforcing officials are the vital parts of any civilization. The only question in my mind was whether the law could be made to function soon enough to handle the outlaws. It couldn't now, so the pressure of time was the important factor, and I was certain it was what had brought the whole business to a head.

Munro seemed a little reluctant to continue. He fiddled with his pipe, trying to get it going, and, when he did, he glanced at Bowers, then at the Dunn boys, and finally brought his gaze to my face. If I read the sign right, the four of them had made an agreement, and the only reason they had come to me was to persuade me to enlist in their project.

"Our plan is to hit the outlaws without warning," Munro went on finally. "If anyone talks and the word gets out as to who is involved, we'll fail. Now, this is the plan. Jerry Bowers will pick three men from his area he knows he can trust, and work down the Yellowstone. I'll take three men and come down the Missouri from the mouth of the Musselshell."

He nodded at me. "Dave, you and the Dunn boys and another man I'll send you will start from the Dunn Ranch and work down the Yellowstone to Jones Point. I understand there are no hide-outs below that until the Yellowstone runs into the Missouri. You may think that four men in each party is not enough to clean out these nests where the outlaws have holed up, but I think that four good men can do the job if they move fast and use good judgment."

I didn't argue with that. Surprise would be the big factor. Most outlaws I had known were not very smart. Unless they were warned, they would not expect this kind of organized effort to root them out. It was true that, if the word got out, everyone would fail. Speed. A quick attack. It could be made to work. I shook my head. No, that wasn't the sticker for me. It simply graveled the hell out of me that Munro assumed I'd go along.

"Jeff," I burst out, "by God, I just don't savvy this! You're not asking me. You're telling me. You know damned well that a lawman can't get mixed up in this."

He nodded. "I should have talked to you before, Dave, but we didn't have our plans made till last night. We need you to run this end of it. I told the others you'd help. I guess you'll have to turn your badge in. Tell 'em you're going to be away for a few days. They'll be glad to give you your job back when you finish this chore."

"We need an experienced man to take charge," Sam Dunn said.

His brother nodded. "We ain't cowards, and we'll do our share of the fighting, but this ain't our line, Dave. We need you."

I sat there staring at Munro and only half hearing what the Dunn boys had said. My heart was churning and my guts were twisted into a big knot, but the funny thing about it was that I knew I'd do it. I wouldn't and couldn't refuse to do anything within reason that Munro asked, and I knew this had to be done one way or another.

Still, I didn't want any part of it. I didn't want to give up my job. I didn't want to leave Miles City. I didn't want to be separated from Sandy, and I wasn't sure how she'd take leaving. Then, for some reason, the thought came to me that maybe I'd been here long enough, that it was time Sandy and I left. There was nothing to keep her here, and now that I thought about it, there sure as hell was nothing to keep me.

"The man I'm sending you is named Mack Russell," Munro went on, as if not even considering the possibility that

I wouldn't take the job. "He's been in our employ for over a year. He earns his money by sending reports to us of who the horse thieves are and what their movements are. He knows the lower Yellowstone as well as any man, so his job will be to guide you, but you're the boss, and don't let Russell forget it."

I still hadn't said I'd do it. They stared at me a moment, waiting, I guess, for me to give them an answer, then Bowers said: "Jeff, he ain't said he'd do it. If he won't, we're going to have to give up the whole shebang."

"Why?" I demanded. "There must be a dozen men better qualified than I am. If you need only one more. . . ."

"That one is the point," Sam Dunn said. "Only a special man can do it. You're that kind of man."

"I didn't know I was that important," I said grimly. "I tell you, Jeff, I don't like it."

"Neither do I," Munro said. "I've helped hang some mighty mean, low-down sons-of-bitches, but I never liked doing it, even when I knew the world would be a better place with them gone."

I thought about that a minute. These men had their own axe to grind, yet the fact was that a hanging was never a pretty act. I could see Munro's point, that he'd been in this kind of a deal not because he liked it, but because it had to be done. I guess I had never thought about how the men felt who had been involved in vigilante action. I suppose they felt the way I did, not wanting any part of it, but knowing the job had to be done.

"A couple more things, Dave," Munro said. "You'll get five hundred dollars for your time, in case you decide to go somewhere else and you're out of work for a while. Russell gets the same. The rest of us are doing this to save our outfits, so we have a stake in doing a good job without getting paid for it. The other thing is that, if you ever want a job from me, you've got it, or if I can recommend you for a job anywhere else, I'll do it."

They were silent again, still watching me. I could not put off answering them. I said reluctantly: "I'll do it."

"Good." Munro rose and held out his hand. "We'll all move on the morning of May Tenth. You be at the Dunn spread the night before so you can leave before dawn on the tenth."

He shook my hand. The Dunn brothers and Bowers shook hands with me. Then, when Munro reached the door, he turned back. "We ain't positive about this, but from what Russell has seen and heard, it seems that Pete Green is the jasper who's organized this bunch. There may be several gangs that have been operating north of here, but Green's is the biggest."

He went out. The others followed, Bowers closing the door behind him. I sat there a long time, staring at the opposite wall. I had given my word, I could not back out now or later, but I had never been pulled in opposite directions as much as I was on this business. I had to tell Sandy something, but, of course, I could not tell her the truth, so I went over in my mind a dozen times what I would say.

As soon as my shift ended at midnight, I went directly to Sandy's place, going along the alley to her back door. Her lamp in the bedroom was lighted, so I knew she had been expecting me. I opened the door and slid into the room quickly and shut the door.

"Good evening, Marshal," she said. "I'm very happy to see you."

She greeted me in all kinds of ways, but she always said she was glad to see me. I didn't say anything until I stood beside the bed and looked down at her. She was wearing a frilly pink

141

nightgown that was new to me. Her black hair seemed blacker than ever against the pillow. Her full lips were parted slightly, the corners of her mouth turned up in a smile.

"Have I ever told you that you are the loveliest woman I have ever seen in bed?" I asked.

"Oh, you're just flattering me again," she said. "I'll bet you tell that to all the women you find in bed."

"No, just you."

She held out her arms to me, and I sat on the edge of the bed and kissed her. When I drew back, I said: "Sandy, I've got to talk to you."

"You sound grim and forbidding," she said.

"I didn't mean to sound that way," I said. "It's just that I've come to a decision. I've had enough of Miles City. I've got to be gone for a while next month, but when I come back, I'll sell my lots, and maybe you can sell this place. Will you come with me?"

"Oh, honey," she said, "don't ask such stupid questions. Of course, I'll go with you. Anywhere. Anytime. And don't you ever think of leaving without me."

"That is the last thing I would do," I said. "Before I came to Montana, I rode through northeastern Oregon. I remember seeing a ranch near Baker City in the Blue Mountains that I liked. Maybe I can buy it. Or one like it. Would you like to live on a ranch? It means a lot of hard work."

"I would like nothing better," she said gravely. "Believe me, honey, almost anything will be better than making dresses and hats for a bunch of critical whores."

I didn't know she felt that way. She had never indicated before that she was not happy here. And she didn't ask me why I was leaving or where I was going. She never did, thinking, I guess, that anything I did was necessary. It was one of a number of things I liked about her.

142

Chapter Twenty

I would be leaving Miles City as soon as we finished the job Jeff Munro had given us. I did not make a decision. I simply knew that was what I would do. Sandy and I could not put our roots down here. If we moved to some distant place where neither of us was known, we could become solid citizens. I think this was in both of our minds, although we never discussed it.

Besides, I was tired of carrying a star, tired of looking out for people and trying to protect them, tired of man-handling men who were stupid enough to get drunk and disturb the peace, tired of knowing every hour of the day that I was a target for any murdering maniac who had it in for me enough to want to kill me.

All of this piled in on me suddenly. I think the reason was that I found upholding the law in Miles City and going out on a lynching expedition were so incompatible that I could not go back to being a lawman. If I were to have any peace of mind in the future, it would come from being a private, law-abiding citizen who had done an ugly but necessary thing.

I took care of two chores quickly before I had time to change my mind. Not that I would have. It was simply a matter of shifting the direction of my life, so there were some things I had to do.

First, I informed Abe Calder and Doc Lewis that I was turning in my star on May 9th. They tried to talk me out of it, even promising to raise my salary, but I told them I had no choice, and let it go at that.

The second choice was easier. I went to Pearly Means and told him to sell my lots, to take any price that was reasonable, that I would be leaving town in a few days. He immediately made me an offer which I'm sure was too low, but it gave me a small profit, so I took him up on it.

He probably resold the lots in a matter of weeks at a big profit, but I never regretted letting him have them. I wanted them off my hands. I was anxious to leave nothing that would hold me back once I was finished on the river.

The day after Munro left, I received the $500 he had promised in the mail. From then on time dragged, and I wished we could have started immediately, but I understood Munro's thinking, that he and Bowers had to have time to return home and organize their parties, and that it was essential for all of us to strike at the same time.

I would have preferred to have kept my departure quiet, but the news got around that I had resigned, so I was asked where I was going and what I was going to do, and why I was leaving Miles City.

I managed to evade the questions, saying I had stayed in Miles City longer than any other town in my life, and now I had to move on. Most of the people understood, because they had drifted around much of their lives and probably would continue to drift. It did seem that people were genuinely sorry to see me go, and, of course, that was gratifying.

Sandy heard some of the talk, I suppose, but still she never questioned me, any more than she had that first night when I had mentioned I would be leaving. I had supper with her the evening of May 8th and told her I was pulling out the next day and might be gone for ten days or more. I didn't really know how long it would take, so I could not tell her anything definite, but I wanted her to have her home sold before I came back.

She laughed. "I'm way ahead of you, Dave. I sold a few days ago to Rosebud. She's going to build a big place and become a madam. She'll give Maggie and the rest plenty of competition, or I miss my guess."

I was surprised, but I should not have been, because Rosebud had always been popular. I'm sure she had made enough money to buy the property and build a house. The surprising element was the fact that she had saved her money. Few whores did.

I moved my personal possessions to Sandy's place. I shook hands with Bill Dillon, who was taking my job. This struck me as being funny. He had been anxious to give the job to me when I came, but now the town had changed and was slowing up, and he was glad to get his old job back.

My intentions were to stop briefly at Sandy's place as I left town, but she held me longer than I expected. She acted as if she might never see me again, so I guess she sensed I was heading out on a dangerous mission. I had been careful not to say anything that would give her that impression, but she felt it just the same.

I tried to pull away from her, but she clung to me, crying a little, and finally she said: "Dave, Dave, please come back to me. Without you there's nothing to look forward to. Just nothing."

When I rode out of town, I told myself I should not have promised anything, but I'd said: "I'll be back. I promise."

The odds were good I wouldn't come back. For the first time since I had given Jeff Munro my word, I had serious thoughts about not going on with it. It seemed stupid to be risking my neck for something that really was not vital to me either way. I knew how much Sandy had done for me, and how much I had done for her. To get killed at this point—I put it out of my mind. I was only torturing myself. I knew very well that I could not turn back.

I reached the Dunns' Rainbow Ranch at dusk. The Dunn

brothers were relieved to see me. I'd had no contact with them since they had walked out of my office with Munro and Bowers, and I suspect they were beginning to wonder if I was going to show up.

I had barely finished shaking hands with the Dunn boys when another man bustled up, a busy kind of man who seemed to be in motion all the time. He said: "I'm Mack Russell." He pumped my hand with great enthusiasm. "I'm glad to see you. We're going to make a good team. You can count on it. We'll hang every one of them thieving bastards."

The familiar stirrings of doubt were in me again. Even more than the time I had met Joe Abbot in Miles City. I didn't like Mack Russell, and I didn't trust him. That was a hell of a note, because I was going to see a lot of the man in the next ten days or two weeks.

"Yeah, I reckon we'll make a good team," I said.

Russell was a lanky man, taller than I was, and about half as thick through the shoulders. He wore a heavy black beard and very long black eyebrows. His eyes were pale blue and, surrounded as they were by his black beard and brows, gave you a weird feeling that they were dimly lighted windows surrounded by complete darkness.

"Sure we will," Russell said with the same hearty enthusiasm. "They've had it their way too long. Well, I've got to go see about the grub. We don't want to starve, do we?"

He walked away, still giving the crazy impression that all the parts of his body were in motion. I looked at the Dunns and shook my head. "How did Jeff ever hire that crazy galoot?"

Ben Dunn laughed wryly. "He's been here for two days, and he's about driven both of us loco. I think Jeff knew what kind of a jasper he was, but Russell knows the river, and none of the rest of us do."

Sam Dunn nodded agreement. "I think he'll be all right,

Dave. All he's got to do is to guide us. He won't sell us out to the outlaws. He ain't got his five hundred dollars yet."

"He must think he's running our outfit," I said.

Sam nodded. "He does."

"And you'll tell him different," Ben added.

"We're taking two pack horses," I said. "No more. They'll low us up, the best we can figure."

"You'd better tell him that, too," Sam said. "He figures to ake four. He says we'll be gone more'n two weeks."

I found him at the storehouse. He had enough grub piled up in the middle of the big room to last a small army a month. I said: "Russell, we're taking two pack horses. See that you don't have any more grub than two horses can carry."

His mouth sprang open as he stared at me. He started to say something, closed his mouth, and swallowed. He said: "Now, you listen to me. I know where we're going and how long it will take. We'll need at least four pack horses."

"You heard me," I said.

I started to walk away, but he ran after me and grabbed my arm. "We may be gone a month. Mister Munro said I was to guide you and make the proper arrangements. If you ain't gonna let me do what I think is right and proper, then I ain't goin'."

"Suit yourself," I said.

His head was tipped back so that the light from the over-head lantern fell directly upon his face. He didn't say anything for several seconds, but I saw his eyes. I had never seen such concentrated hatred in a man's eyes before in my life. I think he would have killed me if he'd known how to do it, but at the moment he wasn't wearing a gun, and no other weapon was handy.

"All right," he said sullenly as he turned away. "Two pack horses it is."

Ben Dunn was waiting outside. He said: "We'll see what the cook can dig up for your supper. We ate about an hour ago."

"That Russell," I said. "He's a back-shooter."

"I believe it," Ben said. "I hope he shoots the right back."

"So do I," I said. "I always figured Jeff was the kind of man who never makes mistakes, but it looks to me like he made a dandy when he sent Russell to us."

"I'll wait and see how good a job he does guiding us before I decide that," Ben said.

I didn't argue with him, but I had already decided. The part that bothered me the most was the fact that I couldn't figure out what Russell was up to. Why did he plan on being gone a month? Nothing that I could think of answered the question, but one thing was sure. I aimed to keep Mack Russell in front of me.

Chapter Twenty-One

We ate breakfast by lamplight, saddled our horses and loaded our pack animals, and were ready to go by the time the first small arc of the sun showed above the eastern horizon. For a moment we sat our saddles, with Mack Russell looking off into space as if he didn't see anything.

"Lead out, Russell," I said sharply.

"Oh, I thought our leader would be the first to ride out," he said innocently, and turned his horse downriver.

I had to struggle to restrain myself. I glanced at the Dunn brothers, who were grinning uneasily. I think they were as embarrassed as I was. Naturally I wanted to pull Russell out of his saddle and remold his face, but I had learned a long time ago that there was a time for violence and a time to hold off, and I knew this was not the time to work Russell over. The time would come. I wasn't sure when or how, but I knew it would come.

We rode hard that day, following the river for a time, then turning into the hills that lay to the west. Spring had come early that year, with more than normal rainfall. We'd had several warm days, and this was one of them. Eastern Montana often had no spring at all, but moved directly from winter into summer, and very often that happened late in what the calendar said was spring.

I enjoyed the ride, because I'd never been in this country before. Normally it was a barren badland, but for a time this year it was bright with yellow daisies, white Mariposa lilies, and crimson vetch. We camped beside a spring that evening, well back from the river, and we heard the frogs croaking all night below us where the little stream from the spring ran a zigzag course toward the Yellowstone.

There was a strange and haunting quality about this country. I guess it was true of all of eastern Montana, but I felt it that evening more than at any other time, maybe because of the job we were here to do. It was certainly on my mind. The Dunns, too, I think, although I doubt that Mark Russell gave it a thought.

I'm not sure what it was that made me feel this haunting quality. Maybe it was a combination of things. The breeze was quite gentle, but it was my guess that most of the time the wind blew down these gulches as if it were trying to move everything that was in its way.

The wind could be killing in the winter, with icy knife blasts, and be nearly as killing in the summer, with its searing, oven-like heat. From the shape of the small twisted pines that grew on the slopes above us, I'd say there were damned few days when the wind didn't blow.

Or perhaps it was the weird blue haze that clung to the hills most of the day, giving them a misty sense of unreality. Or the azure-blue sky and crystal-clear air that enabled a man to see as far as the lay of the land permitted. As the daylight turned to night, the stars came out, and it seemed to me I had never seen so many or as bright as they were that evening.

More than anything else, I think, was the sheer space that was all around us. We were the only people to mar the emptiness. There were animals, of course. We had seen deer that day, and now we heard the coyotes. There would be wolves not far from us, and perhaps elk, and countless small creatures that had shot through the sage ahead of us all day, but no people.

Still, I knew the men we sought were not far from our camp, men who would likely be dancing at the end of a rope in another twenty-four hours. I could not see them now. I could not feel their presence, so for me at that moment we were alone in an empty land.

At a time like that a man's mind runs free and wild. I thought of Pete Green, and I had no worries about hanging him, because he had turned bad. But what if we found Lucky with him? We would not hang her. I promised myself that, and yet I did not know how the others would feel.

The woman was as much an outlaw as anyone. As Sandy had said, she had brought this fate onto herself. Still, I had no stomach for hanging a woman, any woman, Lucky least of all. I could not forget her kindness when I first came into Miles City.

I thought, then, of Sandy, who had come into my life so unexpectedly and so forcefully, my first experience with love. It would be the last. I wanted no other woman. Not that I was by nature any more monogamous than the next man. It was just that I knew she was all there was. Another woman would have nothing more to give me than Sandy had.

Most of all, I thought of myself and my future, and what I would do. I was finishing one chapter. What would the next chapter tell? Strangely enough, I seemed to face a wall, and I could not think beyond it.

That night I dreamed of a rope and a big noose. It settled over me and tightened until I could not breathe. The next thing I knew, one of the Dunns was poking me in the ribs and telling me to wake up, that I was all right.

As we were eating breakfast, Russell said: "There are three hide-outs we're going to hit. The first one is Dolan's Landing. It ain't far from here. We'll tackle it this afternoon. The next one is Lane's Stockade, and the last will be Jones Point. That's the big one, and, if we're lucky, we'll bust the whole damned outfit when we clean it out."

So that was where Pete Green would be. Russell gave me a searching look, his Adam's apple bobbing crazily. He had been reasonably courteous since we left the Rainbow, but he hadn't said anything more than he had to. Now I had a feeling that he wasn't sure how far I could be trusted, but maybe it was my imagination, because I disliked him so much.

"The only trouble is, we may find the first two empty," Russell went on. "With good weather like this, some of them are going to be out after horses. I told Mister Munro we should do this in the wintertime and we'd find 'em all home, but he wouldn't listen."

We wore our horses out that day, climbing steep slopes and sliding back down others just as steep. Russell said the bluffs ran right down to the river, and this was all we could do. Besides, we'd be hidden from any of the outlaws who were still at Dolan's Landing. We could follow a gulch down to the buildings, he said, but it didn't work out that way.

We were in a steep-walled ravine with Russell saying we'd be there in another ten minutes. We reached a sharp turn. The next thing we knew we ran headlong into three men who were riding away from the river.

"That's them!" Russell yelled, and began shooting.

We had no time to ask questions or think about what we'd do. The three men went for their guns the instant Russell yelled, and the rest of us had no choice. It was kill or be killed. We got into the game about half a second after the three men started banging away at us.

In another two or three seconds all of the outlaws were dead. I had a bullet through the top of my hat, and Ben Dunn had a nicked left arm that bled like hell for a while but didn't do any real damage.

We pulled our horses to a stop and sat there a moment, the dust and powder smoke swirling around us. The outlaws' horses whirled and ran back down the ravine. Russell stepped down and began pointing at one dead man, and then another.

"Long John Akins." Russell kicked the body in the ribs, then turned to the next one. "Hambone Riggins." He stood at the third body, his face distorted with fury. "This one's Dunc. I never heard him called nothing else. He was a mean son-of-a-bitch."

He turned to his horse and mounted. "Chances are there ain't nobody else down here, but we'd better be a mite careful. If some more of 'em are around here, they're close enough to have heard the shots."

In about ten minutes we came out of the ravine and were in a lush green meadow. Ahead of us were a cabin, several small outbuildings, and a maze of corrals. No one was around, no horses were in the corrals, no smoke rising from the cabin. Still, we moved carefully toward the buildings, ready to dive for cover at the first sign of trouble. We reached a log shed and reined in behind it.

Russell dismounted. "I'll take a look," he said.

Before I could stop him, he'd lunged around the corner of the shed and sprinted toward the cabin. "The damned fool," Ben Dunn said angrily. "If anyone is inside, Russell's a dead man."

Somehow I couldn't see Mack Russell as a hero, so I decided he must have known that only the three men would be there. Still, I wasn't able to figure any way he could have known for sure. I couldn't take away from him the fact that his quick shooting had stopped the three outlaws.

On the other hand, there was no way to tell who had shot who, but I did know that one of the outlaws was falling before I got my gun into action. I didn't doubt that Russell's first shot and yell had surprised and disorganized the outlaws, and I wound up deciding that, if he had not reacted as quickly as he did, we would have been a hell of a lot worse off.

A moment later Russell stepped into view around a corner of the cabin. "No one here," he called, "but we'd better check the other buildings!"

We did, and found them deserted. I stepped into the cabin. Not much there in the way of furniture: a stove, a table, and three benches. Even the grub had been cleaned out. We pulled saddles off the outlaws' horses and turned them loose. The Dunns did not recognize the brands, but Ben said that didn't prove anything. They could be Canadian horses, or from the Dakotas.

"Plenty of brands we don't know," Ben said. "All you can count on is that they move Montana horses out of the territory and fetch some in from a long ways off. They're the ones they'll be riding, so if they're caught, nobody can prove they stole 'em."

One thing was plain. Russell had a personal hate for the men we had killed. Especially the one he'd called Dunc. Later that evening when Russell had left the campfire, I mentioned this to the Dunns.

"No doubt about it," Sam said. "It came out pretty clear in them two days he spent with us. He had this store for a year or more on the other side of Jones Point, you know, and it seems the outlaws abused him, made fun of him, and pulled all kinds of tricks on him.

"He just grinned and stood it, he said, but we're guessing that was why he turned spy for Jeff Munro, and it's why he wanted to take this trip. He's got plenty of personal reasons for cleaning these bastards out."

I didn't like it, and the more I thought about it, the less I liked it. Russell could be using us to get his revenge for the ill treatment he'd received, but how did we know the men we were killing were horse thieves? Today we'd had no choice, because if we hadn't shot fast and straight, we'd have been killed.

As far as I was concerned, any man found here was an outlaw, proof or no proof, because there was no reason for a man to be in these old wood-chopping camps unless he rode with the horse thieves. Personally I was glad it had been a shoot-out. At least we hadn't strung them up.

We burned the buildings and rode downriver at dawn the next day. Three days later we came to Lane's Stockade, and almost the same thing happened. This time it was two men. We rode through a thick grove of cottonwoods, coming into the open about fifty yards from the old stockade that had been built years ago for protection against the Indians.

The two men were chopping wood between us and the stockade, apparently not seeing us until we were in the clearing. They didn't stop to palaver. One of them yelled—"The stranglers!"—and dropped his axe and grabbed up his gun from where it lay on the ground. The other man was only a second behind him. They got in the first shots, but they were wild. We knocked both of them over, not even getting a bullet through our hats this time.

"That's only five," Russell said. "We're after about forty of 'em. That's the number Mister Munro has on his list."

"We won't get 'em all," I said.

"No," Russell admitted. "Our big haul will be at Jones Point. Might be as many as a dozen men there. Also one woman. Most of the brand-changing is done there."

"Four of us against a dozen?" I said. "We're not taking on that kind of odds."

Russell turned his smoldering eyes on me. He said bitterly: "I had my store. Remember? I know every rock and tree and hole in the ground there is. We can do it."

We had to try, I thought, and again I asked myself why I

was risking my neck in a fight that wasn't my affair. I dreamed about Sandy that night. I was in bed with her, kissing her and holding her in my arms, but a heavy rain woke us and we moved into the stockade. I didn't sleep any more that night, but lay on my back thinking about Sandy.

In the morning we burned the buildings and started down the river, the clouds hanging low over the hills. We wore our slickers all day, because the rain pounded away at us until late afternoon, then the clouds disappeared and the sun came out.

One more day, I thought, and then Jones Point, a dozen hardcases against us. Pete Green would be among them, and Lucky, too. Funny thing about time. You keep thinking that the tomorrow you don't want to see will never come, but the tomorrow was almost here, and I still didn't want to see it.

That night I dreamed about the noose again. This time it was bigger than ever, and, when it tightened around me, I could not breathe. I tried to scream for help, but I could not make a sound. Then Sam Dunn was shaking me, yelling at me: "What the hell's the matter with you, Dave?"

I couldn't tell him, so I turned over and said: "Nothing." But I did not go back to sleep.

Chapter Twenty-Two

After breakfast the next morning Russell picked up a stick and drew a map for us in the dirt. He said: "Jones Point is a peninsula that sticks out into the water. The boats used to pull into the bank at the end of the point to load up with wood. The buildings are back a piece from the river. There's one big log building where they eat. Green and his woman live in it. She does the cooking for the whole outfit.

"Then there's two cabins where the men sleep. Besides them buildings there's some sheds for horses, and one storehouse. My idea is to leave our horses a mile or so from the point and work up close during the night. They eat breakfast early, close to camp, so we'll have 'em all in the big building at one time. If we're lucky, we can wipe 'em out without showing ourselves."

I shook my head. "Suppose they fort up in the main building?" I said. "There's no way we can get them out."

"I'll get 'em out," he said coldly. "You three be ready to smoke 'em down when they leave. That means you're gonna have to get close enough to shoot straight when the light's still purty thin."

"How?" I demanded.

He glared at me. "You don't trust me to do what I say I will, do you, Harmon?"

"Oh, hell," I said. "We've come this far and killed five men. I've got to trust you, but I've also got a right to know how you're going to pull this off."

He glanced at the Dunns, the corners of his mouth working, then he said: "All right. The windows are all on the front wall of the main building. The only outside door is between 'em. I aim to get on the back side and start a fire. I was hoping the rain didn't reach this far, and it didn't. That building will be as dry as tinder. They're gonna come barreling out through that door. You'll be facing it from the corrals. All you've got to do is to knock 'em off. It'll be like shooting fish in a barrel."

I didn't say anything, but it looked like a long shot to me. How could he get that big a fire going so that they'd have to leave the building and run into our guns? It was up to him, and, since I couldn't think of a better scheme, I kept my mouth shut.

He made some more marks in the dirt to indicate where the sheds were, then showed the location of the corrals. "You can reach the corrals before any light shows. They're close enough to the front door for you to knock the horse thieves over when they show."

"If it's that big an outfit," Sam Dunn asked, "won't they have a guard out?"

Russell laughed. "Sure they will, but I'll get him. You know, Green's a smart *hombre,* and so are some of the others, but the part that's gonna get 'em all killed is that they think nobody's got the guts to come in after 'em.

"They're a proud, arrogant bunch of sons-of-bitches. They used to stand at the bar in my store and talk about how they'd wipe out any posse that showed up. They just don't take the kind of precautions that they should. It's my guess the guard will be asleep when I slip a knife into his brisket."

"All right, Russell," I said, "we'll play it your way, but it looks damned risky to me. I don't savvy why you want to take this big a risk. If they spot you back of that building, you're a dead man."

He looked at me a long moment, a strange, savage expression coming into his face that made his pale eyes glow. He said: "Harmon, you don't have no notion of what it's been like to live with them bastards the way I have. I had a good store when the boats were running, but when the horse thieves moved in, I was in hell. They insulted me and humiliated me and made me the butt of their god-damned jokes. I'd rather die trying to whip 'em than to go on living and remembering what they done to me and knowing I never tried to square accounts with 'em."

I nodded. "I savvy."

I thought about it as we rode out that morning. It struck me that he had a lot more reason to risk his hide on this job than I did. I tried to put Pete Green into this situation, but he didn't seem to fit. Sure, he could be arrogant, but being a jokester who would humiliate a man like Mack Russell didn't jibe. But men change. Too, the truth was, I never really knew the man. I don't think anyone ever really knows a professional gambler, and maybe that is the reason some of them are successful gamblers.

We rode through an open country that day, weaving back and forth between flat-topped buttes partly covered by small pines. We stopped at noon and cooked a meal, Russell saying we would be too close to the point at suppertime to risk a fire.

Before it was dark, we topped the bluffs that at this point sloped to the river, and looked down on Jones Point. We were close enough to see the layout of the buildings. They were exactly as Russell had said, except that there was a fine grove of cottonwoods on the point, most of them south of the buildings. There were horses in the corrals, a lot of them. Even this late in the afternoon, men were working with them, apparently changing brands, as Russell said they did here.

We rode on until it was nearly dark, then tied our horses, ate a cold meal, and moved on foot, Russell leading, the rest of us following. There was a full moon, which made walking easier, but it would also make it harder to work in close to the buildings as we had planned.

We were on a good trail, probably the trail used by the horse thieves when they moved the stolen stock to and from Jones Point. Tall brush shaded the trail, so we were reasonably well covered. The trail itself was shadowed, so we couldn't see what we were stepping on, and all of us fell several times. It's a miracle we didn't sprain at least one ankle.

Sometime after midnight, about two or three I think, we smelled tobacco smoke. Russell put his back to me, signaling me to stop, and I passed the signal to the Dunns. Russell moved on ahead. Presently I heard a man say: "Who is it?"

"Russell. I've got a pack train back on the trail a piece. I thought I'd better come on and let you know who I was before you cut loose."

"Move up so I can see you," the man said.

Apparently Russell did. The next sound I heard was a strange gurgle, the sort of sound a man might make if he had a knife in his chest. A moment later Russell was back with us. "It ain't far now," he whispered.

In another ten or fifteen minutes we were out of the brush and into the cottonwoods. Russell stopped us. He whispered: "We've got an hour or more before daylight. You work on up to the corrals. They're straight ahead. Don't move or say anything until I start the ball."

He disappeared, circling away from us through the trees. "He's either a brave man or a fool," Sam said.

"He's crazy," I said, "but he's no fool."

I had never known a man driven by the thought of revenge as much as Mack Russell. Maybe he had suffered enough to make a man crazy. One thing was sure. He had lived with his dream of vengeance so long that now, having reached the point in time he had dreamed about, he was willing to do anything to achieve his goal.

We worked our way toward the buildings, very slowly and carefully, using the shadows as much as we could. When we reached the corrals, we startled some of the horses, but I suppose there were enough wild animals around so that it was not unusual for the horses to get spooky. At any rate, no one showed up to investigate.

By the time it was dawn, we were hunkered down at the edge of the corral nearest the biggest shed. We didn't have much protection except what the corner of the corral or the shed would give us, but we'd be all right until it turned full daylight. I judged the shed was built of logs, and, if the fight turned out to be a drawn-out affair, the shed would be a reasonably good fort.

Now the time seemed inordinately long. A man came out of one of the cabins to relieve himself, then went back in. Presently smoke began pouring out of the chimney of the big building. Green stepped outside and filled a bucket at the pump, and went back in. From what I could see at this distance in the thin light, he had not changed. I wondered about Lucky and if she was still wearing her heavy veil.

Another ten minutes passed, the light slowly deepening. Two men left one of the cabins and headed straight for us. I hadn't figured on this. They'd see us before they got halfway to the shed, but I wasn't a man who could shoot them down in cold blood. As it turned out, we didn't have to.

A moment later one of them saw us and yelled: "The stranglers have got us surrounded!" He yanked his gun from its holster, but I cut him down before he could fire. The second man started to run back to the cabin, but the Dunns knocked him off his feet before he'd gone ten yards.

Then all hell broke loose before we were ready for it.

Chapter Twenty-Three

Men poured out of both cabins. Pete Green ran out of the main building and dived back in when I threw a shot at him that must have been close. About the same time, I smelled smoke and saw a thick column billowing up from the other side of the big building.

I crouched at the corner of the shed, and the Dunns were at the edge of the nearest corral. All three of us were firing as fast as we could pull our triggers. Some of the outlaws were confused and started toward us, then changed their minds as we cut down two of them. They darted back into the cabins, and others bolted toward the river. We fired at them, but I don't think we hit any of them. They made it to their boats and pushed out into the stream. In a short time they were out of sight.

Russell had fired both cabins, so it was only a matter of minutes until the remaining horse thieves were forced outside. Two of them had guns in their hands and came at us on the run. I guess they figured it was better to die with bullets in their brisket than burn to death or dance at the end of a rope. We obliged them before they had covered half the distance to where we were.

Two more had their hands up. I yelled: "Hold your fire!" The Dunns stopped shooting, but I wasn't sure where Russell was or what he was doing. The men who moved across the yard toward us were scared. They had a right to be. I don't think they doubted for a moment what was going to happen to them.

Pete Green was still in the main building, shooting at us,

but he must have been a very nervous man about that time. Besides, we weren't giving him much to shoot at. One end of the log structure was burning, the flames leaping twenty feet above the roof. I don't know how he stayed in so long as he did. A moment later a woman ran out, coughing, a handkerchief held to her mouth.

"Come out before you burn to death, Pete!" I yelled.

The woman wore a heavy black veil, so I couldn't see her face, but it was Lucky. It had to be. She came straight toward us, still coughing. She was about halfway across the yard when Green ran outside, firing as he came. By the time he caught up with Lucky, his gun was empty. He kept on running past her straight toward us.

We were standing now and had moved forward away from the shed and corral. When Green was about twenty feet from me, he threw his gun at me. It sailed over my head by about three feet. I guess he recognized me at the same time, because he yelled: "So it's you, Harmon!"

He was on me in two more long strides. He tried to hit me, but I ducked the punch and slugged him once in the belly. It was enough to take the fight out of him. He bent over and sat down, his head tipped forward as he struggled for breath.

"Russell," I called, "we've got them. Where are you?"

He came into view between the two burning cabins. He yelled: "What about them that got to the river? Didn't you see 'em?"

"Sure we saw them," I said. "We couldn't get all of them."

The two men who had surrendered were standing in the middle of the yard, their hands up. Lucky ran on past me to Green, who sat with his back to the shed. She knelt beside him, asking: "You all right, Pete?"

"Sure," he said, still having trouble breathing. "I'm fit for hanging."

"That's exactly what you are fit for," I said. "Sam, you and Ben go take a look at the horses. Maybe you'll recognize some of the brands."

Russell had come on up to us. He was furious. He said: "By God, Harmon. I flushed 'em into the open for you. Looks to me like you could have shot 'em."

"I didn't see you do any shooting," I said. "Six of them are lying dead there in front of you, and we've got three for hanging. What does it take to satisfy you?"

"All of 'em," he snarled. "All of 'em."

Green got to his feet and stood with his back to the shed. He asked: "Four of you is all?"

"That's all," I said.

"Well, now," he said coolly, "so the marshal has turned hangman. Is that your notion of justice?"

"You're a poor one to talk about justice," I said, motioning for him to join the other two. "Stand together, all three of you."

Russell was looking at Green and then at the two men in the middle of the yard and then at Lucky. "Damn it, Harmon, you can't count past three. I say we've got four to hang."

"No, it's you who can't count." I had expected this from him, but still it made me sore. "We'll hang no women."

"She's as guilty as the men," he said. "I say she hangs with 'em."

I'd had more than enough of Mack Russell. I'd been stuck with him ever since we'd left Rainbow Ranch, but I didn't aim to be stuck much longer. I stepped toward him, my gun covering him instead of the three prisoners. I said: "I'll have no trouble with you, Russell. You keep pushing me and I'll kill you just as quick as I would them. Quicker, maybe. You're trash, and not all of them are."

Green laughed contemptuously. "You're right for once,

Dave. Trash. That's all he ever was. Left here to bring back supplies for his store, he said, but, instead, he fetches the stranglers. Turncoat! That's Mack Russell for you."

Russell was looking at me as if he didn't believe he'd heard me say what I had. He wheeled away as the Dunn brothers came toward the corrals. "About twenty Rainbow horses here, at least," Sam said. "I don't know all the brands, but some of 'em are from ranches north of Miles City. Looks like they just brought in a big band."

Russell grabbed his arm. "Sam, this bastard who's been giving us orders threatened to shoot me. He says we ain't hanging the woman. I say she hangs the same as the men. She's just as guilty as they are."

I grabbed him by the shoulder and whirled him around and hit him on the chin. It was a good blow that hurt my arm all the way back to the shoulder, but there was a lot of satisfaction in it. With the exception of Abbot I had never enjoyed hitting a man so much before in my life.

"Don't call me a bastard again," I said, "or it'll be more than my fist that hits you."

Sam nodded. "You'd better listen good, Russell. Dave's right. We didn't come here to hang a woman."

"Civilized, law-abiding men," Green said in that same contemptuous tone he'd used before. "I thought all lawmen believed in a trial by jury."

I didn't even answer, but it struck me as interesting that men who break laws are the first to try to use them to protect themselves when they're caught. I had noticed a fine, well-limbed cottonwood about twenty yards to the south. Smoke was drifting toward us from the burning buildings, the fire crackling and snapping as heat pushed at us.

"Sam, you and Russell go fetch in the horses," I said. "These men can use some time to make their peace with their

Creator. Ben, see if you can find some ropes."

Russell was on his feet, rubbing his chin. He didn't say a word, but wheeled and started walking away. Sam said in a low tone—"Watch your back, Dave."—and caught up with him.

Ben Dunn disappeared into the nearest shed. I motioned toward the cottonwood. "Move over there," I said. "You can sit down or stand. If you want to pray, get at it."

"It'll take more than a prayer to save our necks," Green said. "When a lawman like you forgets his duty and decides to stretch our necks, there ain't nothing we can do."

He was bitter. I looked at him a long moment, trying to see the smooth, clean-shaven, well-dressed gambler I had known in Miles City. This wasn't the same man. He was dirty, his face was covered by a week's growth of stubble, there was a rip in his white shirt that was so soiled it was far from white, and the pride and the dignity that had been his in Miles City were gone.

He was just another outlaw now, a little smarter maybe, but the same caliber as the two men beside him. They were run-of-the-mill hardcases like the ones who used to hang around Joe Abbot's ranch.

"Move," I said, and jerked my head toward the big cottonwood.

They walked to the tree and sat down. Green lay back on the grass and stared at the sky. The other two sat up and looked at me, still scared and apparently not knowing what to do or say. I suppose they had left their guns in the burning cabin. At any rate, they weren't armed now.

Still, I hadn't searched them, so when Ben Dunn returned with the ropes, I said: "Better go over our prisoners in case they have some hide-out guns on them."

"Yeah," Ben said. "I wondered about that. The woman, too."

Lucky was still standing at the shed. I motioned to her. She was wearing a common, faded gingham dress, nothing like the expensive dresses she had worn at Wolf's Saloon, but as she came toward us, I remembered how she used to walk with shoulders-back pride that I had always admired. In this way she had not changed.

"I'm sorry, Lucky," I said when she reached us, "but we've got to look you over for a gun."

"I suppose you want me to take my clothes off," she said.

"No." I shook my head. "It'll be enough if Ben here feels of you."

"I've had better men than him feel of me," she said scornfully.

Ben grimaced. "I dunno about that, ma'am, judging from the looks of these jaspers you've been running around with."

He ran his hands over her, then examined the three men. He said: "They're clean, Dave."

"Get the ropes ready," I said.

Ben nodded. "I reckon I can tie a knot that'll do the job."

Green didn't stir, but now the other two began to beg for their lives. "Shut up," Green snapped. "You've lived like men. Now die the same way."

Lucky turned to me. "I want to talk to you, Dave."

"Go ahead," I said.

She shook her head. "Alone."

"Can you keep an eye on the prisoners, Ben?" I asked.

"Sure." He was working on the ropes about thirty feet from the three men. Now he drew his gun and laid it on the ground beside him. "Maybe they'd rather get shot than hang. If they jump me, that's what'll happen."

I backed away toward the shed, still watching the three men and wishing that Ben was farther away from them than he was. I said: "This is far enough, Lucky."

167

I don't know if she had the same thought I did or not, but I suspect she did. She said: "No, Dave. I don't want Pete to hear."

"He won't if you talk low," I said.

She gripped my right arm. I shook her loose at once, convinced that she did have the same idea. I said: "I've got to keep that arm free, Lucky. If they jump Ben, I'll kill them."

She dropped her hand and began to cry. It was a strange feeling, talking to a woman with a dark veil over her face so that I could not see her features and, therefore, had no idea of what she was thinking. I didn't say a word. I just let her cry, my eyes on the three men under the tree.

When she could talk, she said: "You know what I'm going to say, don't you, Dave?"

"No."

"I think you do. I'm going to remind you that you owe Pete one life. I told you that a long time ago."

"The debt's been paid," I said. "I paid it the day he killed Joe Abbot."

That was when the two men made their move.

Chapter Twenty-Four

Pete Green lay in the grass, his head propped up on one arm. He was watching us with cool indifference. The thought struck me that he was a man who had all of life he wanted and now welcomed death.

The other two men remained on their feet, looking at me and Lucky, then at Ben, who was having trouble with the knot. He swore and glanced up at me, saying: "I don't know how to tie a. . . ." They jumped him before he finished the sentence, one man going for the gun on the ground, the second one diving at Ben.

Lucky couldn't possibly have set up the maneuver with the two men, and yet it seemed as if she had. The instant the men moved, Lucky grabbed my right arm again, this time with both hands. Ben was preoccupied with the knot, so that he was slow to move, and for an instant I had the terrible feeling that I was having a nightmare in which I was paralyzed and I was going to be destroyed because I couldn't move.

I tried to shake off Lucky's grip, but I couldn't. I hit her on the side of the head with my left hand, a hard blow that sent her reeling. I started shooting the instant my right arm was free. The man who went after Ben got to him just as his fingers closed over the butt of the gun. The outlaw kicked Ben under the chin, slamming his head back and making him drop the gun. He spilled over backwards as the second man scooped up the gun and whirled to fire at me.

My first bullet drilled the man with the gun through the head just above the nose; the second got the other man as he jumped on Ben, one booted foot driving into his belly and knocking the wind out of him. The bullet caught the man in the side and spun him half around. My next shot nailed him in the chest. He must have been dead by the time he hit the ground.

I wheeled on Lucky. "You expected me to quit trying?" I had no right to cuss her out. Sure, I expected her to go on trying. I would under similar circumstances. I said: "Maybe I should let Russell hang you?"

"I wish you would," she flung at me. "What have I got to live for if you hang Pete?"

"Hell, you've got your own life," I said.

"No," she said miserably. "I've had no life from the time Joe Abbot shot me."

She walked to where Green lay, still apparently amused by the drama he had just watched. Maybe he wished now he had joined the other two. I don't know. I couldn't tell a thing from the expression on his face.

Lucky sat down beside Green and cradled his head in her lap. She said to me: "Get away from us. We've got a right to some privacy."

I turned to Ben, who was sitting up, one hand on his belly. His face was white. He said: "By God, Dave, they almost turned the tables on us. Seemed like you was slower'n molasses with your gun."

"I was," I agreed. "I was wrestling with Lucky."

"Ungrateful bitch," he said. "Maybe we ought to hang her."

"We won't," I said, "but right now I feel like I'd enjoy doing it." I picked up Ben's gun from the ground and handed it to him. "You watch them. I'm going to look for some shovels."

I tried the sheds and then the storehouse and found several shovels and picks. Here, too, were great quantities of food, saddles, blankets, and various odds and ends. I discovered the answer to a question that had been bothering me. How had Russell got such a roaring fire going as soon as he had?

Here was a row of coal-oil cans on one shelf. Three were gone from the middle of the row. It was a reasonable guess that Russell had doused the back of the cabins and the main building. As dry and old as the logs were, the coal oil had been enough to make them burn quickly and fiercely.

Carrying the shovels and picks, I returned to where Ben was sitting, the rope in his lap. He held the noose up for me to see and shook his head. "I dunno, Dave. This sure ain't no professional job of knot tying, but I think it'll do the job."

I stopped dead still and stared at the noose, my heart pounding. Suddenly I realized that it was the noose I had dreamed about, and I remembered that in my dream the noose had been around me so tightly that I could not breathe. Sweat broke through the pores of my face as I thought about what Lucky had said: *You owe Pete one life.*

"What's the matter with you?" Ben demanded. "Don't you think it'll do the job?"

"Sure," I said. "It's fine."

I walked away. This had been digging away at my conscience from the day I had left Miles City, but now, seeing the whole affair in the light of cold logic, I realized that nothing had changed. Pete Green was as guilty as hell. We had caught him with stolen horses. He had held up at least two stages and had murdered two guards and one passenger. Maybe more. If we took him to Miles City, he would certainly hang. There were two differences—the extra days he would live and the fact that someone else would do the hanging.

No, I could not save Pete Green if I wanted to. The Dunns agreed with me about hanging a woman. Russell would agree, because he had no choice, but, if I tried to keep Green from

171

hanging, all three would fight me if I let it come to that.

Well, I wouldn't let it come to that. I couldn't. I had known I would face this situation when I agreed to come. There had been no turning back once I had given my word. There was no turning back now.

Sam Dunn and Russell returned with our saddle horses and the pack animals. They saw the bodies of the two men who had jumped Ben and asked what happened. After we told them, Russell said sourly: "Only one man to hang." He would, I thought, have preferred a limb full.

"Only one," I said.

I think he wanted to say something about hanging a guilty woman, but he took another look at my face and didn't. All he said was: "Use my horse."

I nodded. I walked to where Green and Lucky sat under the big cottonwood. "Time," I said.

They rose. Lucky turned her back to me and lifted the veil so that she could kiss Green, then she turned away and walked to the storehouse, went inside, and closed the door.

We wasted no more time. Russell brought up his horse, we tied Green's hands, and I helped him into the saddle as Ben tossed the rope over the biggest limb and anchored the other end to a nearby tree.

Green looked down at me, his face as expressionless as ever. He said: "Look after Lucky, Harmon."

"I'll see that she gets to the railroad," I said.

Ben adjusted the knot and tightened the noose.

I asked: "Have you got any last words, Pete?"

He looked at me, and I thought he was close to smiling. He said: "Why, yes, I do, Dave. You can go to hell."

I gave the horse a clout on his rump with my hat, and he lunged forward. Green was yanked out of his saddle and dropped. I'm sure he was killed instantly. I knew that sometimes a man lived until he was slowly strangled, and I was afraid that might happen.

His body turned back and forth and swayed a little. I walked away and was sick. Only Russell stood staring at Green's body, his lips parted, an expression of sheer ecstasy on his face. I felt like hitting him.

A short time later Ben cut the rope and laid Green beside the two men who had jumped him a short time before. I picked up a shovel. "We'll put them in one grave," I said. "Let's get started."

We worked a good part of the day digging a long trench in the sandy soil. We didn't stop to eat. I don't think anybody felt like it. Late in the afternoon Ben said: "We're about done. Why don't you head out with the woman, Dave? It's gonna take you a little while to get to the railroad. There ain't no boat left here to cross the river."

"We'll take the horses to Miles City," Sam Dunn said. "We'll drop our horses off at Rainbow and let the sheriff have the rest."

"I'll saddle a horse for her," I said.

"She rides that little bay yonder," Russell said. "The one in that first corral."

I saddled the bay, then I said: "Nobody talks. Is that understood?"

"Sure, we understand," Ben said, a little sore because I had even suggested that they might talk.

"You, Russell," I said. "If you open your mouth about what has happened here today, I'll cut out your tongue."

"I believe you would," he said sullenly.

I led the horses to the storehouse and went in. Lucky was sitting in the back of the room, her head down. I said: "We'll throw some grub in a sack and start. I'm taking you to the railroad."

She had removed her veil, but the light in the storehouse was so thin I could not see her face. Now she dabbed at her eyes and dropped the veil over her face. She asked: "Is it over?"

"It's over," I answered.

She found a sack and filled it with enough food to last through tomorrow. She said: "There's a ferry down the river a piece. We can reach it by tomorrow noon." She returned to where she had been sitting and picked up two saddlebags. She said: "I didn't save anything from the house, but there's a few things out here I want to take."

We went outside. I called: "Burn everything before you leave!"

"We'll do it!" Ben yelled back.

Lucky was in the saddle. I mounted, glancing at her. She was staring straight ahead. I couldn't see her face through the black veil, so I had no clue about what she was thinking or feeling, but certainly she was leaving a part of her life here, and she must have been very much aware of it. I sensed something else, too. She did not know what lay ahead of her, but she was not afraid.

Chapter Twenty-Five

We had ridden about half a mile when Lucky pointed to a log building beside the trail. It had a small corral behind it, a hitch rail in front, and a sign above the door that read: **STORE**.

"That's Mack Russell's store," Lucky said. "We traded with him because it was handy. Nobody liked him. He was an animal. He still is."

"What did he do that makes you say that?" I asked.

"A lot of things," she said, "but there was one time I'll never forget. He was waiting for me one evening when I left the house to go out back. The boys were gone after horses, and nobody was left but Pete. He'd gone to bed. Russell tried to attack me. I scratched him and bit him, but he'd torn most of my clothes off before I could scream enough to wake Pete up."

"What did Pete do?"

"He almost killed Russell. I had never seen him so mad. He told Russell he would kill him if he ever touched me again, and I think he would have."

"Did he ever try again?"

"No. Pete scared him enough so he never came around me after that."

"He said he was the butt of jokes and he was humiliated."

"How could a man like Mack Russell be humiliated?" she demanded. "Sure, he was the butt of jokes. He was so stupid he never caught on to what they were up to."

She didn't say anything more until we made camp another five miles down the river. After supper I said: "Pete said Russell was a turncoat, but he was never one of Pete's outfit. I

175

don't see how Pete could accuse him of that."

"He didn't have to bring you and your stranglers back here, did he?" she snapped. "He made a living off Pete and his men for years . . . then he helped hang Pete."

I didn't tell her that Russell had been paid by Jeff Munro for information about the horse thieves for the past year. I thought it would be too much. She had reason enough to hate Russell without knowing that.

Lucky was silent for a long time. We sat beside the fire, listening to the water lap against the willows, then she said: "When you first came to Miles City, Dave, I would have moved in with you if you'd given me a chance."

"I know that," I said, "but it's like I told you. I never take another man's woman."

She ignored that. I was not even sure she heard me. She went on: "I told you then I didn't know if Pete loved me. At that time I brought him luck. I was good to look at. I was a pleasure to him in bed." She turned to stare at me, and added with more feeling than I had ever heard in her voice: "I know now he did love me all the time. It was just that he wasn't a man to show it or say it. He was like all gamblers. He had trained himself to hide his feelings. Most men would have thrown me out after Abbot shot me. I'm a horror to look at, and I certainly didn't bring Pete any more good luck, but he kept me, Dave. I . . . I guess we were closer after the shooting than before."

"I'm glad," I said. "You deserve to be loved."

"Because I've had a lot of unhappiness in my life?" she asked. "Or because I loved Pete?" She didn't expect an answer, and I didn't give her one. She was hunched forward, staring at the fire, and then added slowly: "I'm not sure I did love Pete. I've always looked out for Number One. I've often asked myself if I ever loved anyone or anything in my whole life. I honestly don't know." Again she was silent for a time, then she said thoughtfully: "I think I had wanted someone to take care of me. I'd taken care of myself so long."

"What will you do now?" I asked.

"Go to some new town," she said. "Bismarck, maybe. I'll buy a house if you don't take my money away from me. I'll be known as the Veiled Madam. I'll even have one room with a mirror on the ceiling for the carriage trade."

She had said there were a few things in the storehouse she wanted to take with her. I realized now that those few things were greenbacks and gold coins, probably some of the loot she and Pete and the others had taken in their stagecoach robberies. For a moment I considered taking the money from her, but I couldn't do it.

I had no way of knowing that it was the stagecoach money she was carrying. Besides, my job was to get her to the railroad. I was no longer a lawman. It was not my duty to restore stolen money. Anyhow, I didn't know to whom it belonged.

"Why did Pete go bad?" I asked. "He killed men in those hold-ups that he didn't need to."

"I know," she said tonelessly. "I've seen him kill men on the point for no good reason. I don't know why except that he seemed to hate everyone and everything except me after Abbot shot me. He was about broke then. His luck had been bad for a long time. He tried to borrow from John Bains and Eli Whitcomb, but they wouldn't lend him a penny."

"He didn't have any collateral," I said.

"He told me that wasn't necessary," she said. "His word should have been enough. He was a gentleman. Then, after the shooting, he said Abbot wouldn't be convicted, that he'd get free with all his money, and it was up to him to square accounts. Of course, after he had shot Abbot, there was no way out except to turn outlaw. He said he had the name, so he might as well play the game."

He could have gone somewhere else, changed his name, and lived his own life, because nobody around Miles City was going to hunt him for the murder of Joe Abbot. But he didn't know that, and he wasn't one to find out.

The thought struck me that Pete Green must have had a mean and cruel streak in him, just as Joe Abbot had. It had been covered up as long as he could make a living gambling, but once that bubble had been punctured, there was nothing left except to go bad.

"He could have got a job," I said. "He was a smart man."

"Too smart," she said bitterly. "He was not a man who could have led a normal, law-abiding life. A job was the last thing he wanted. He said only the stupid worked, that the smart men worked other men, just as Bains used the bank and Whitcomb used the law. They let other men do the work, and they skimmed off the cream." She yawned and stretched. "I'm going to bed, Dave."

I brought her saddle and blanket to the fire. She lay down and pulled the blanket over her and fell asleep almost at once. I didn't. I sat beside the fire and stared at it, and thought about the three people who had changed my life so much since I had come to Miles City. Pete Green, who had saved my life and who had been hanged by me; Jeff Munro, who had sent me on this hanging trip; and Sandy Lennon.

It was pleasant to sit there and think of Sandy. I would see her soon, and we would go away. I would probably never see Jeff Munro again, and, for the first time since I met him, I realized I did not want to see him. I wasn't sure why, except that his ways were not my ways. He was older than I was; he would never change with the times, and I knew I would.

When I did go to sleep, I saw Pete Green's being yanked off his horse, the rope snapping taut as his weight came down

178

hard on it, the grotesque twist of his head, the horrible expression on his open-mouthed face, the swaying of his body like a ghastly pendulum.

I woke trying to scream, but I was unable to make a sound. I finally got up and threw more wood on the fire and sat beside it for a long time. Once more I went to sleep, and this time I woke with my lungs bursting, the noose around me so tightly I could not breathe. Again I built up the fire and sat beside it until the eastern sky turned red.

We ate a quick breakfast, neither of us wanting to linger. We reached the ferry before noon and crossed to the other side, where we sold Lucky's horse and saddle in the little railroad town above the ferry, then we waited for the first eastbound train.

Lucky bought her ticket for Bismarck. When the train pulled in, she stood for a moment beside the steps that led up into the coach, staring at me. She asked: "How's Sandy?"

"Fine," I said.

"You're really in love?"

"I am," I said. "I think she is, too."

"I know she is," Lucky said. "She was in love with you after the first time she saw you. You two are the lucky ones, not me." She turned toward the coach as the locomotive whistled, then swung back. "I guess I should thank you for not hanging me, but how can I thank a man who hanged Pete?"

This time, when she turned around, she climbed the steps and went into the coach. The train banged into motion. I strode to my horse, swung into the saddle, and rode upriver, wondering if I had done Lucky a disservice by keeping her from hanging alongside Pete Green.

Chapter Twenty-Six

I rode back to Miles City very slowly, making camp early each afternoon along the Yellowstone. I wanted to see Sandy. I wanted to leave Miles City. I wanted to start a new life, but still I did not hurry.

What I wanted most was to make peace with myself, to be able to sleep through the night, to stop having that damned nightmare of the noose tightening around me until I could not breathe. Even when I was awake, I felt as if someone had his boot heel hard against my gut.

This was the first time in my life that I was able to answer my own questions on a mental, rational level, and still be unable to meet them emotionally. That had to be what was happening, or I would not go on having the nightmare; I would not find sleep so illusive that I would stay awake half of each night as I had been doing now.

I have heard it said that time is the great healer. I found it to be true. I began to enjoy making camp, being by myself, eating solitary meals, then watching the day go and the night move in, seeing the scarlet of sunset fade about the western bluffs, hearing the mournful call of coyotes from some distant rim, and feeling the vast emptiness that enveloped me.

Sometimes I heard the shrill cry of a train whistle. I had no idea of distance, for sound travels farther than a man expects in this empty land. Or I might hear a night bird calling as it swooped down out of the dusk toward me, and then wheeled and fled. I heard the faint whisper of the river as it rolled on toward the Missouri, the crackling of the fire, the sizzle of bacon as I cooked my supper.

In spite of these varied sounds, the feeling that came to me was of silence, of a vast and deserted land. I met no one. If I talked aloud, it would be to myself or to my horse, and I did not doubt that, if any other human being had been close enough to hear, he would have been quite sure that I was completely loco, and he would have left me alone.

The problem was the same one that had dug into my conscience from the time I had agreed to go on the vigilante expedition, of being, as the horse thieves had accused me, one of the stranglers. I had been a lawman, but now I had broken the law to hang a man without a legal trial. I suppose the conflict was made worse by the fact that the man we had hanged had saved my life that first day I was in Miles City.

There was no use to keep going back over what had happened, because nothing had changed. Yet, slowly, the change did come. Somehow I came to grips with the fact that what was done was done. Right or wrong, it was behind me, and now the only thing that mattered was to know that Sandy still loved me, that she was looking forward to another place, another life. Before I reached Miles City, I found that I could sleep all night, and the nightmare failed to come.

Still, even though I had made peace with myself, I was not prepared for what I met when I rode into Miles City and left my horse in the Ringer and Johnson livery stable.

The stableman said—"Howdy, Harmon."—and gave me a smirking, sidelong glance, as if he knew I'd been up to something I shouldn't and he knew what it was. "How was she?"

"She?" I stared at him, honestly having no idea what he was talking about. "What she?"

"Oh, don't act innocent," the stableman said impatiently. "I'm talking about Pete Green's woman. Everybody in town knows what you've been doing. I can tell you that a lot of us remember how you used to look at her in Wolf's Saloon when

Green was playing cards there."

So that was it! I had trouble breathing. I knew too well that people are inclined to believe the worst about another human being, man or woman, but I had never thought it would happen to me.

I wanted to throttle the man, to beat him to death, but he wasn't the guilty one. I had an idea who had spread the story, but that wasn't enough. I said: "Go on."

He was a little scared then. He backed away from me as he said: "Now, don't fly off the handle, Harmon. You couldn't keep a thing like that secret. We never thought you'd show up here. You resigned your job, so after you strung Green up, we figured you'd just keep on going with her, now that you had her. Of course, they say she ain't no beauty after she got that scarred face, and she keeps it covered with a veil, but. . . ."

I couldn't hold myself back any longer. I grabbed him by the shoulders and shook him till his teeth rattled. "Who's been telling this?" I demanded.

"Why, Mack Russell," he said. "He was with you, wasn't he? He saw what happened, didn't he? He helped bring the horses to town that didn't belong to the Dunns. He said you'd cleaned out the horse thieves from here to Jones Point and. . . ."

"Take care of my horse," I said, and wheeled and strode out of the stable.

I looked in five saloons before I found Russell. I don't know how long he'd been back in town or how many times he'd told his story. Apparently he had assumed I'd left the country for good, just as the stableman had said. At least he had no idea I was here.

He was standing at the bar with his back to me. He was talking to several man, Eli Whitcomb and John Bains and some cowhands I didn't know. He was saying: "It was the damnedest thing. You wouldn't have believed it if you hadn't seen it, but there Green was, hanging from that cottonwood limb, and there was Harmon on the ground in front of the storehouse screwing Green's woman right in front of all of us. She wasn't fighting him off, neither. I tell you. . . ."

I had stopped just inside the batwings. Now the others had seen me, and I guess their expressions caused Russell to turn around. He froze for a moment, then he licked his lips and began to tremble. He took a step toward me, spit drooling down his chin. He hesitated, took another slow step toward me, and then he dropped to his knees.

"I was lying to 'em, Harmon," he said. "I didn't think you'd ever come back to Miles City. I told everybody you'd take that woman and keep on riding. She was what you wanted, wasn't she?"

I didn't say a word, but my hand was on the butt of my gun. Except for the time I had given Joe Abbot a beating, I had never wanted to kill a man so much in my life, but I knew he didn't have the guts to draw on me. If I killed him, it would be like killing a man who wouldn't fight, and I couldn't do that. I knew it, but Russell didn't.

He starred crawling toward me, and then he began to cry. "Don't kill me," he babbled, the tears running down his cheeks. "I'm sorry. I'm saying I lied to 'em. They don't believe me. You ask 'em. They'll tell you they knew I was lying."

I looked at them, and then at the men sitting at a poker table, Doc Lewis and Abe Calder and several other townsmen. *They did believe Russell.* I was as sure of that as I was sure of anything. After living here all this time and risking my life to give them a safe town to live in, I was shocked that they would believe a story like this from a man like Mack Russell.

I whirled and strode out of the saloon and down the street

to Sandy's house. I had intended to leave Miles City, and that was what I was going to do, but I had a bitter taste in my mouth, a taste I never thought I would have in this town. Now, more than ever, the only thing that mattered to me was what Sandy thought. She must have heard Russell's story. If she believed it. . . . But I could not bring myself even to consider that possibility.

She was in the kitchen when I stepped into her front room. I called: "Sandy!"

She had heard the door and was already on her way toward me. She cried out: "Dave, it's been so long. I've been worried."

She ran to me, and I guess I ran to her. I don't really remember. All I know was that she was in my arms and I was kissing her, and the bitter taste was no longer in my mouth. Let them think what they wanted to. Maybe it was my imagination that made me think they believed Russell's lies. I didn't know, and suddenly I didn't care.

Sandy was crying, and I was tasting her tears. I held her hand against me, her face against my shirt front. When she tipped her head back, she said: "I'm so glad you're back safe. I've heard the stories Russell has been telling, and I suppose there is some truth to them about the hanging."

"We hanged Pete Green," I said, "and I took Lucky to the railroad. Do you believe what Russell said about me and Lucky? I suppose you've heard that, too."

"Of course, I didn't believe it," she said. "How could I? Why would you want her when you've got me?"

"I heard him talking just now," I said. "I had a feeling that the men who were there did believe his story."

She shook her head. "No. I don't think so. He's been telling the story to anyone who would listen. I don't think people believed him. Not your friends, anyhow."

I knew then that it was more important to me than I wanted to admit about whether the Miles City people believed Russell, but what she said helped. I wanted to believe her.

"Are you ready to leave?" I asked.

"I've been ready for a long time," she said. "I've bought a horse to ride, and I've made a riding outfit to wear. I want nothing more from this town. This is all behind us. I love you, Dave."

"That," I said, "is all I really wanted to hear."

About the Author

Wayne D. Overholser won three Spur Awards from the Western Writers of America and has a long list of fine Western titles to his credit. He was born in Pomeroy, Washington, and attended the University of Montana, University of Oregon, and the University of Southern California before becoming a public schoolteacher and principal in various Oregon communities. He began writing for Western pulp magazines in 1936 and within a couple of years was a regular contributor to Street & Smith's *Western Story Magazine* and Fiction House's *Lariat Story Magazine*. *Buckaroo's Code* (1947) was his first Western novel and remains one of his best. In the 1950s and 1960s, having retired from academic work to concentrate on writing, he would publish as many as four books a year under his own name or a pseudonym, most prominently as Joseph Wayne. *The Violent Land* (1954), *The Lone Deputy* (1957), *The Bitter Night* (1961), and *Riders of the Sundowns* (1997) are among the finest of the Overholser titles. *The Sweet and Bitter Land* (1950), *Bunch Grass* (1955), and *Land of Promises* (1962) are among the best Joseph Wayne titles, and *Law Man* (1953) is a most rewarding novel under the Lee Leighton pseudonym. Overholser's Western novels, whatever the byline, are based on a solid knowledge of the history and customs of the 19th-Century West, particularly when set in his two favorite Western states, Oregon and Colorado. Many of his novels are first-person narratives, a technique that tends to bring an added dimension of vividness to the frontier experiences of his narrators and frequently, as in *Cast a Long Shadow* (1957), the female characters one encounters are among the most memorable. He wrote his numerous novels with a consistent skill and an uncommon sensitivity to the depths of human character. Almost invariably, his stories weave a spell of their own with their scenes and images of social and economic forces often in conflict and the diverse ways of life and personalities that made the American Western frontier so unique a time and place in human history.

Wayne D. Overholser
WILD HORSE RIVER

The Wild Horse River is the dividing line in San Marcos County, with the ranchers on one side and Banjo Mesa on the other. But the small ranchers and the Banjo Mesa residents got together to elect Jim Bruce as county sheriff, an act of defiance and a slap in the face to Holt Klein, owner of the huge K Cross ranch. When the owner of Gray's Crossing, a small ranch over the river, is murdered, Klein insists all the evidence points directly to the Banjo Mesa people. But Jim Bruce isn't convinced that everything is as neat as it seems. Could Klein be trying to set one side against the other? Asking questions like that will make the sheriff even less popular with Klein, and Holt Klein is a dangerous man to cross.

WHEELS ROLL WEST

Wayne D. Overholser

Wayne D. Overholser, winner of three Spur Awards from the Western Writers of America, weaves his usual spell of excitement and emotion in these two short novels, appearing in paperback for the first time. The title novel tells the story of a wagon train making the perilous journey from Ohio to Colorado. Before they arrive at trail's end, a Pueblo gambler and his gang arrive, declaring that if the settlers want to continue they will have to pay—with everything they own. And in "Swampland Empire," Riley Rand arrives in Blue Lake Valley and announces he owns the entire area. But some of the local residents don't take too kindly to the news. . . .

Ken Hodgson
FOOL'S GOLD

Jake Crabtree has been searching for gold for years. But he's pretty lazy and his luck has never been good, so it's no surprise that his search hasn't turned up much. Until now. Coming out of winter hibernation—when he usually goes on one long drinking binge—Jake learns that his benefactor, Dr. McNair, is at death's door. The doc's last request is to be buried on the claim that he shares with Jake. It's when he's digging the doc's grave that Jake finally strikes a rich vein of gold. But Jake's about to find out that gold brings with it a lot more than wealth. It also brings a whole passel of trouble and a pack of back-stabbing varmints!

Dorchester Publishing Co., Inc.
P.O. Box 6640
Wayne, PA 19087-8640

_5436-1
$5.99 US/$7.99 CAN

Please add $2.50 for shipping and handling for the first book and $.75 for each additional book. NY and PA residents, add appropriate sales tax. No cash, stamps, or CODs. Canadian orders require an extra $2.00 for shipping and handling and must be paid in U.S. dollars. Prices and availability subject to change. **Payment must accompany all orders.**

Name: _____

Address: _____

City: _____ State: _____ Zip: _____

E-mail: _____

I have enclosed $_____ in payment for the checked book(s).
CHECK OUT OUR WEBSITE! www.dorchesterpub.com
____ Please send me a free catalog.

VOICES
IN THE HILL
STEVE FRAZEE

With his eye for historical detail and unique ability to see into the hearts of his characters, Steve Frazee captures the very essence of the American West. In these five stories, collected for the first time in paperback, Frazee draws on his own experiences to bring his writing to vivid life. The title story tells of Riordan Truro, an old man who's been working in the mines so long that he understands the story behind every shift, every groan in The Hill. His fellow miners think he's touched in the head, but only Riordan knows The Hill has an ominous warning for those who work in its depths. Will he be able to convince everyone to get out before it's too late?

Dorchester Publishing Co., Inc.
P.O. Box 6640   _____5484-1
Wayne, PA 19087-8640 $4.99 US/$6.99 CAN

Please add $2.50 for shipping and handling for the first book and $.75 for each additional book. NY and PA residents, add appropriate sales tax. No cash, stamps, or CODs. Canadian orders require an extra $2.00 for shipping and handling and must be paid in U.S. dollars. Prices and availability subject to change. **Payment must accompany all orders.**

Name: _____

Address: _____

City: _____ State: _____ Zip: _____

E-mail: _____

I have enclosed $_____ in payment for the checked book(s).